THE TOWERS
OF ILLICA

STAR OF DELTORA

1. Shadows of the Master
2. Two Moons
3. The Towers of Illica
4. The Hungry Isle

THE TOWERS OF ILLICA

EMILY RODDA

First American Edition 2017
Kane Miller, A Division of EDC Publishing

First published by Omnibus Books a division of
Scholastic Australia Pty Limited in 2016.

Cover type by blacksheep-UK.com
Design and graphics by Ryan Morrison Design.

This edition published under license from
Scholastic Australia Pty Limited.

For information contact:
Kane Miller, A Division of EDC Publishing
PO Box 470663
Tulsa, OK 74147-0663
www.kanemiller.com
www.edcpub.com
www.usbornebooksandmore.com

Library of Congress Control Number: 2016934239

Printed and bound in the United States of America

1 2 3 4 5 6 7 8 9 10

ISBN: 978-1-61067-527-7

CONTENTS

1 - Secrets to Keep

The Isle of Tier was feeding. The hidden reef that circled its shore had made short work of the fishing boat it had snared. Sand and forest rippled as the island consumed splintered wood, tangled nets, drowned rats and tubs of rotting fish with equal, silent relish.

The fishing boat had been drifting, deserted. Who knew why? Sea serpent attack, a freak wave, a drunken fight in the night ... There were many ways frail humans could come to grief in the Silver Sea.

The King of Tier brooded, hunched amid the glories of his gem-studded cavern. Crystal bowls of crab claws, honey cakes and berries red as rubies floated in the air before his throne, but his stomach churned at the thought of food, and the bowls remained untouched.

The King had faced the perils of the Silver Sea himself, many times, in his previous life. No one knew better than he did how luck at sea could turn, how weather could change, how one bad decision could mean the difference between life and death.

The ship that had been haunting his mind for weeks was sailing the Silver Sea at this very moment. He could sense her, because she was nearer to him now and drawing closer every day. He could almost see her white sails swelling, hear the waves slapping against the prow that bore the name *Star of Deltora*.

She was a fine ship—strong as well as beautiful. But the Silver Sea was treacherous, and this, the King dimly recalled, was the season for storms. Anything might happen before the *Star of Deltora* reached safe harbor once more. A tearing gale, a raging sea, a broken mast, a panicking captain—and all aboard the ship might perish, as the crew of the fishing boat had perished.

Britta might perish …

Britta, whispered the wraiths that flitted like shadows around the cavern walls. *Your daughter, Larsett. Bone of your bone. Flesh of your flesh …*

The King did not hear them. His mind had filled with visions of Britta drowning in dark, salty water, her long hair trailing like seaweed as her lifeless body sank down, down to the ocean floor …

Sweat broke out on his brow. His heart seemed to swell till it knocked against his ribs.

With a shock he became aware that the wraiths were pressing close to him, moaning dolefully. They had felt his agitation. Shielding his mind in haste, he tightened his grip on the ancient black diamond Staff that stood beside his throne, its tip buried deep in the island's earth.

As his mind calmed, he told himself that it was useless to fret over things he could not control. The Staff of Tier could create and destroy. It could heal all injuries and cure all ills. By its power, the Hungry Isle was a living thing that could move, conceal itself, and stalk prey. By its power he, the King of Tier, was mighty, safe even from the envy of the fearsome Lord of Shadows. But he had learned long ago that though the Staff could sense events happening at a distance, it could not change them. He could do nothing to alter the fortunes of the *Star of Deltora*.

The ship would sail safely, or it would not. Britta would survive the voyage, or she would not. He could only wait in hope and dread, like any other man.

The thought was strange, and bitter.

"Get away!" he snarled at the fawning wraiths, and noted uneasily that though they cringed back a little, they did not retreat. They were still slaves to the Staff, but his power over them was waning. It had been waning ever since he had given in to his fears and sent some of them to bring him news of Britta.

That had been a mistake—a grave mistake. He had sent those shades to spy, to answer the questions that had been tormenting him. He had not dreamed that they would feel the girl's bond with the Staff and so become attached to her.

But they had. In their thin, pale way, they had. Returning with what was for him the worst of news, they had infected the others with their sick doting. And then, before he could stop them, they had rushed back to Britta—to Britta on the *Star of Deltora,* sailing the Silver Sea with Mab, the Trader Rosalyn.

Sailing to Maris, Two Moons and Illica—the same three ports that he had visited on the quest to find the Staff. The same ship, the same ports … this could not be merely chance!

And as the King of Tier squirmed and scowled on his throne, the suspicion entered his mind that Mab had chosen to repeat his voyage on purpose to taunt and insult him.

It must be so. It *was* so! He ground his teeth. Anger boiled in his stomach and burned behind his eyes. So this, all this, was Mab's fault!

Vain, scornful old woman with her dyed hair and painted face! So proud to be the great and wealthy Trader Rosalyn, mistress of a vast fleet! So determined to cling to power! So willing to defend the odious, unfair rules that her Apprentice—her heir—must be chosen by contest, and must be female!

And now, having been forced at last to hold the famous contest, compelled to take the finalists on the trading voyage that was to be their final test, Mab was soothing her wounded pride by thumbing her nose at him!

A great surge of rage welled up in the King of

Tier. He bellowed in fury. His eyes flamed. Fire gushed from his roaring mouth. The bowls floating before him exploded in a shower of crystal shards. Charred food scraps sprayed the cavern walls that were echoing with the wails of the wraiths.

He came to himself slumped forward on his throne, trembling, sweating and weak. And slowly it dawned on him that his rage had been for nothing.

He had allowed his fears and memories to confuse him. Mab could not be mimicking his last voyage on purpose. She did not know that the *Star of Deltora* had stopped at Illica. No one knew. The visit had been by night, and in secret. He was the only one left alive to tell of it, and the ship's log was at the bottom of the sea.

The King of Tier made himself breathe deeply and evenly. He straightened, firming his lips, turning his mind away from his error.

Mab was not taunting him deliberately, perhaps. But still, she was to blame for this disaster. It was Mab who had delayed choosing her Apprentice so long that Britta had become old enough to enter the contest. It was Mab who had allowed Britta to become a finalist, stupidly unaware that the girl was the daughter of the man despised as Del's greatest traitor since the time of the Shadow Lord.

Most of all, it was Mab who was bringing Britta closer to Tier—closer every moment. Too close, and the Staff might sense Britta's bond of blood with the man whose hand now held it fast, the man who had told the Staff his name and proclaimed himself its Master. It might begin calling to her.

And if it called to her, she would come.

The King shuddered. That must not happen! It must not!

The wraiths were crawling from the walls, creeping back towards him across the scorched cavern floor, moaning and whispering. They could feel his fear, and it unsettled them more than his anger had done. They could not understand it. Soon they would begin asking questions.

Why would Larsett, Master of the Staff, not be glad to have his daughter with him? they would ask. What better fate could befall Britta of Del than to become, in time, what they were, and dwell on the Hungry Isle, in thrall to the Staff, forever?

Over and over again they would ask. How could he answer them?

The King forced the numb fingers that grasped the Staff to flex then tighten once more. He squared his shoulders and raised his head, almost groaning with the effort. The foreboding that was weighing him down felt as heavy as a gravestone.

★

Meanwhile, Britta was prowling the *Star of Deltora,* looking for a place where she could be alone. Wraiths flitted around her, lovingly watching all she did, but she was not aware of them. They were as invisible to her as they were to everyone else. Only the cat Black Jack could see them, and he took care to keep his distance. The crew feared Britta for other reasons.

Laboring before a sluggish wind, the *Star* was plowing slowly towards Illica. Haze filmed the sky, holding in the sticky heat. After weeks at sea the island of Two Moons had been left far behind, but the memory of what had happened there still hung over the ship like swampland mist.

The entire crew had witnessed Britta's arrival at the Two Moons jetty, very late and plastered with swamp mud. Every soul on board knew that she had been in the forbidden center of the island. Everyone had seen the strange mark on her brow, the amber-colored stain that the Two Moons shore men had called in dread "the mark of Tier."

Britta had cleaned herself as best she could, but no amount of scrubbing would wash off the mark. It had faded a little, but that was all. In desperation she had snipped off some of her hair to give herself bangs that covered the stain completely, but the stares and whispers had not ceased. Wherever she went, the ship seemed full of eyes peering at her suspiciously or quickly turning away.

Her stubborn silence about her adventure in Two Moons was no doubt making things worse, but Britta told herself that it could not be helped. There was not a soul on board she could talk to freely. She had too many secrets to keep—more now than ever.

As if I did not have enough already, she thought ruefully. And she pressed her hand to the pocket of her skirt where her two newest secrets lay hidden—a little clay doll that was far more than it seemed and, wrapped in her handkerchief, a precious sunrise pearl.

If only she could lose herself in study, learning as much as she could about Illica, where the pearl was to help her make the most important trade of her life! But she had given up on that. After hours in the reading room, combing every book in the section devoted to the trading ports of the Silver Sea, she had found only the same brief, basic facts about Illica, repeated over and over again.

It was torture staying cooped up in her hot cabin. So Britta prowled, seeking out every quiet place she remembered from her childhood games with the model of the *Star* that her old friend, Captain Gripp, had made.

But people were everywhere—from the ship's boy, Davvie, peering fearfully from the broom pantry to Crow the bosun, glowering in the traders' dining room. Britta had almost given up in despair when a new idea came to her. There was one place she had not tried—a place so obvious that she could not imagine why she had not thought of it before.

The cargo hold!

Britta knew that as a contest finalist she had no business going into the hold, where her rivals' Two Moons purchases were no doubt stored. But it had not been expressly forbidden, and in any case who would know? There were two ways into the cargo hold. The one through which goods were loaded was on deck and clearly visible. But the other, much smaller, was below, in an out-of-the-way corner beyond the reading room.

Wreathed in flickering shadows, Britta threaded her way through a maze of passages till she reached her goal. There was the cargo hold hatch, just as she remembered it from Captain Gripp's model. Eagerly, she pulled the hatch open, revealing the top of a ladder. And the next moment, with no idea what awaited her, she was creeping down the ladder into darkness.

2 - The Iron Box

It was stuffy in the cargo hold, but cooler than anywhere else Britta had been and, best of all, it was deserted. With luck, Britta thought, she would not be disturbed here. Unlike the storage hold, where the food and water supplies were kept, the cargo hold was usually left to itself once the ship had left port.

Britta perched on the lowest rung of the ladder, closed her eyes and for a moment just listened to the creaking of the ship and the muffled, rushing murmur of the sea. The sounds soothed her. The darkness seemed to enfold her. It was as if here in the belly of the *Star* she was safe—as safe as she had felt as a child in her father's arms.

The memory had drifted into her mind before she could stop it. It clung there, prickling like a burr. Britta shook her head angrily and opened her eyes. How many times had she sworn to forget her father—

forget what he had done, forget that she was living a lie? Why had thoughts of him spoiled the first real moment of peace she had enjoyed since leaving Del?

The dimness of the hold was no longer comforting. Suddenly it seemed thick with whispers, and the heavy air seemed to be moving around her, brushing her skin and raising the hairs on the back of her neck.

For the first time in days, Britta remembered the tale that the ship was haunted by some evil presence. Her own problems had driven that earlier fear from her mind, but now it came back to her with full force. The *Star* had been dogged by dread ever since the mysterious Keeper of Maris refused to allow her to drop anchor in his domain. Everyone knew that many in the crew would have deserted in Two Moons if Mab had not offered them double pay.

The Keeper senses a fearful presence on your ship … the odor of death is at its heart, and we do not want it here.

The flat voice of the Maris messenger echoed in Britta's mind. She licked her dry lips.

Mab and Captain Hara had scoffed at the rumors and the fear, and so had Kay, Mab's healer. Hara had not even bothered to have the ship searched. But if something monstrous *was* lurking on the *Star of Deltora,* what better place could there be for it to hide than here, in the shadows of the cargo hold?

Britta stood up slowly, her skin crawling. She almost turned and scurried back up the ladder, out of the whispering dark. But something prevented her.

Something would not let her run.

Perhaps it was pride. Perhaps it was stubbornness. Perhaps it was ... loyalty. The *Star of Deltora* had once been Britta's ship—*her* ship, as well as her father's—or so she had felt in her heart. Long ago, she had made herself face the bitter knowledge that once he was within rowing distance of the Hungry Isle, Dare Larsett had taken the landing boat and left the *Star* to drift. Dazzled by the fabled Staff of Tier, Larsett had betrayed the *Star* as callously as he had betrayed his crew, his country and his family.

Britta was not going to do the same. She was not going to flee from any part of her ship, abandoning it to the darkness.

But fear still fluttered in her chest, and her common sense told her that she should not explore the hold alone. As things were, she could not ask the crew for help, but she should at least ask one of the other contest finalists to search with her.

Jewel of Broome was the obvious choice, but Jewel was irritated because Britta had refused to talk about what had happened in the Two Moons swamp, even in the privacy of the cabin they shared. Sky of Rithmere owed Britta a favor, but he was out of her reach. After being unmasked as a male, Sky was no longer a contest finalist but a lowly deckhand at Bosun Crow's beck and call.

And Britta could just imagine what Vashti would say to the idea of searching the cargo hold. Even if she and Vashti had been friends, as they certainly were not, well-bred Del traders' daughters were far too ladylike to visit the working places of a ship, fit only for the crew.

In any case, Britta remembered uneasily, it might not be a good idea to be alone in this out-of-the-way place with any of them—even Sky. Someone had attacked her in Del. Someone had drugged her in Two Moons. Until she knew who that secret enemy was, she could trust no one.

Then it suddenly occurred to her that she could have company of a kind, if she wished. She unbuttoned her skirt pocket and drew out the little clay figure she had carried away from the Two Moons swampland. The goozli stood stiffly upright on the palm of her hand, its arms by its sides, its head slightly tilted. As she peered at it in the dimness, its small eyes blinked.

"Well, goozli," Britta whispered, "it is just you and me, it seems."

The goozli shrugged, as if it could not see why she would need another companion. And Britta realized that in fact she did feel better. The oppressive shadows seemed to have drawn back. The whispers had become less.

"But there is something here, goozli," she said aloud. "Something ... wrong. I can feel it."

The goozli nodded and bounced impatiently on her hand. Wondering if she was doing the right thing, Britta bent and put it down. Instantly it scuttled away, dodging past a small wooden crate marked "Vashti of

Del" and disappearing into the dark.

Britta felt a sharp stab of panic. "Goozli!" she called softly. "Where are you?"

There was a moment's thick, heavy silence. Then, with a faint pattering sound, the little clay figure was back. It jumped onto the toe of Britta's left boot, bounced off again, then trotted a few steps away from her and paused, looking over its shoulder.

Plainly it wanted her to follow it.

Her heart thudding hard, Britta moved slowly forward, her hands stretched out in front of her. The light filtering down from the deck above was behind her now, and until her eyes adjusted to the dimness she had to strain to keep the goozli in view. But the little creature never darted so far ahead that she lost sight of it, and when at last it stopped, she could see what it had found.

Standing against the back wall of the hold, bedded in thick dust, was what looked horribly like a narrow metal coffin. A length of rusty iron chain with an open padlock lay tangled at its base. Its long black lid was covered in spiderwebs and rat droppings, but the words painted upon it in white were still plainly visible.

Britta stared down at the box. Her heart, beating so hard just a moment before, seemed to have stopped. Her skin was prickling. Her mind was seething with hissing voices, and suddenly she could hear what the voices were saying.

The Staff! they were whispering. *Ah ... the Staff was here—can you not feel it? Open! Open! Open!*

Hardly knowing what she did, Britta tugged at the lid of the box. It was heavy—far heavier than she had expected. But suddenly she felt that nothing was more important than that she should be able to lift it. Every other thought was drowned out by the chant that beat in her ears.

Open! Open! Open!

Gritting her teeth, Britta heaved the lid with all her strength. Abruptly it flew back, crashing against the wall of the hold. For a split second Britta gaped down into a pool of weirdly glowing light, at the padded base of the box, at the long, glimmering groove left by the dangerous treasure that had once lain there. Then she was staggering back, clapping her hands over her ears as a tumult of sound exploded in her mind, as her heart seemed torn from her chest, as moaning shadows swirled before her eyes ...

She came to herself lying where she had fallen, covered in cold sweat and trembling in every limb. The gale of sound had gone. The shadows had drawn back. A hand's breadth from her nose stood the goozli. Its hands were on its hips and it was peering at her gravely.

"I am—all right," Britta whispered. Shakily she sat up. Her stomach lurched as she saw that the lid of the box was shut once more.

She looked back at the goozli. Rather smugly, it tapped its chest and bowed.

Britta swallowed. "*You* shut the box? But ..." Her voice trailed off. She had been about to say that she had not thought a little clay figure would be strong enough to push the heavy lid down, but had realized in time that the goozli would find this insulting.

"Thank you," she said weakly instead. "Thank you, goozli."

She crawled to her feet. She felt as feeble as if she had just risen from her bed after a bad illness, but gradually her mind cleared and she was able to try to think about what had happened. She could only imagine that she had experienced some sort of brainstorm created by shock and fear.

Plainly, the black box had once contained the Staff of Tier. And even after eight long years, traces of the Staff's evil power lingered inside it, just as the Staff's shape could still be seen imprinted on its padded base.

What a fool she had been to open it! But why in the nine seas was it still here, where her father had left it? Why had Mab not ordered that it be removed when she took over the ship in the name of the Rosalyn fleet?

To keep the memory of Father's treachery fresh in her mind, perhaps, Britta thought grimly. Or was it just to show how little she cared? That would be like her.

Whatever the case, the box had been in the *Star*'s cargo hold since the time of Dare Larsett, and the ship had never been forbidden landing in Maris before. So the box was not the cause of the Keeper's warning, which remained a mystery.

The goozli was beckoning. Gratefully Britta followed it back to the ladder, back to the light. She did not look over her shoulder at the iron box. She did not sense the wraiths flitting silently behind her, their feverish excitement quelled now that the box was shut once more.

She had crawled out of the hatchway and was turning to close it after her when she heard a sound and whirled round.

Crow was standing a few steps away from her, staring fixedly at her forehead. He was so close that she could smell the reek of sour sweat and rum that seemed always to hang about him.

"Crow!" Britta managed to say. "You startled me!" Thanking her lucky stars that she had put the goozli back in her pocket before leaving the hold, she casually stood upright. With all her might she fought the urge to touch her bangs and make sure that they still covered the mark of Tier.

"What were you playing at down there?" Crow muttered, showing the whites of his eyes. "You people aren't supposed to go prying into the cargo hold. An' how'd you find this hatch anyway?"

"That is none of your business!" Britta snapped,

too rattled to try to soothe him. "And I was doing no harm. I simply wanted some relief from the heat."

Crow grunted disbelievingly. She tossed her head and left him, feeling his eyes burning into her back as she walked away.

3 - Hidden Treasure

Britta scurried back towards her cabin, taking all the shortcuts she knew. She wanted nothing more than to climb into her bunk and pull the covers over her head. It came to her that she was like a hunted animal making for its burrow, and suddenly she longed for home.

Pictures of her mother and sister serving in the shop, of Captain Gripp sitting by the window of his cottage on Del harbor, flickered in her troubled mind. But most of all she thought of Jantsy, who by now would have finished his work at the bakery and might soon be walking by the River Del, thinking of her.

If only Jantsy were here! If only she could tell him what had happened in Two Moons, tell him what she had just seen and heard in the cargo hold. What a relief it would be to spill out all her fear and confusion to Jantsy, who understood her so well, who would not judge her, who would comfort her and help her make sense of it all.

But these were idle thoughts. Jantsy was far away and could not help her—no one could help her. Britta swallowed the burning lump that had risen in her throat and hurried on. Her spirits rose a little as she neared the cabin. Hot and stuffy as it was, she would at least find peace there. But as she rounded the last corner she saw Sky of Rithmere just turning away from her door.

Britta stopped abruptly, but it was too late—Sky had seen her. She forced herself to walk on. Playing with one of the little ornaments fastened to his dangling braids, Sky leaned against the wall of the passage and waited for her, smiling slightly. As she reached him, his face changed.

"What has happened to you?" he asked. "You look as if you have seen a ghost!"

I have seen worse than that, Britta thought, but she forced a smile. "Oh, it is nothing," she said lightly. "I ran into Crow, that is all. As you can imagine, it was not exactly a pleasant meeting."

Sky did not return the smile. "Take care with Crow, Britta," he said in a low voice. "Keep out of his way. For Hara he puts on a show of being an ordinary rough sailor, but behind Hara's back he is a brutal, greedy bully. I can testify to that, I assure you, after serving under him these past weeks. Crow is dangerous—and he fears you because of that mark on your forehead."

"Then he is an ignorant fool!" Britta snapped, feeling the blood rush into her face and furiously smoothing her tumbled bangs back over her brow. "Sky, I am very tired. Did you want something of me? Or were you looking for Jewel?"

Sky's eyes went blank. She could almost feel him withdrawing, like a turtle shrinking back into its shell. When he spoke again, the familiar, insolent drawl was back. "Jewel is on deck. I came to tell you something—a small return for the favor you did me in Two Moons."

"The *favor* of saving your life, you mean?" Britta shot back, more sharply than she had meant.

Sky shrugged. "My offering is small enough in comparison, I admit, but it is better than nothing."

At that moment, they both heard the sound of footsteps approaching from the direction of the reading room. Sky stiffened, and for the first time Britta remembered what trouble he would be in if he was found in this part of the ship, what a risk he had taken in coming to find her.

"Look in the Sea of Serpents section," Sky muttered, poised to run. "Second shelf from the bottom, behind *A History of Dorne*."

Then he was gone.

Britta hesitated, torn between retreating to her bunk as she had planned and going straight to the reading room to find out what his odd advice had meant. Curiosity won the battle and she turned away from the cabin door only to see Crow appear around the corner she had so lately come around herself.

Crow stopped dead when he saw her. His eyes bulged. "How'd you get here so fast?" he growled. When Britta did not answer, he squinted past her, down the empty passage, and licked his lips nervously. "Who were you talking to?"

"No one," Britta said hastily. "Excuse me, please."

As she edged past him the bosun shrank back as if she was the one who smelled bad, and again she felt him watching her till she was out of sight.

Her heart was still racing when she let herself into the reading room. No one else was there, and quickly she obeyed Sky's instructions, crossing to the bookshelf marked "Sea of Serpents" and looking behind the three weighty volumes that made up *A Short History of Dorne*.

And there, pressed flat against the back of the shelf, was a thick book with a soft brown leather cover. Britta pulled it out and her heart bounded as she saw the title printed on the front.

A Trader's Guide to Illica

"Sky, you rogue!" Britta exclaimed aloud. "You found it first and hid it!"

But she was too pleased with her find to be truly angry. She carried the book to the reading table and began leafing through it, becoming more elated by the moment.

A Trader's Guide to Illica was exactly what she needed. It was packed with facts about Illica, its people and its customs. Greedily Britta scanned the pages, stopping to read now and then when a particularly interesting heading caught her eye.

ILLICA'S "SECRET" HISTORY

Illica is easy to defend, being almost completely surrounded by high cliffs and hidden rocks. Ships must pass through a narrow gap in the cliffs to reach the one safe harbor. It is not surprising, therefore, that in ancient days the island was a pirate stronghold, used as a refuge at one time or another by every pirate ship in the Silver Sea. For centuries it was the scene of greed, cruelty and drunken, bloody battles between the crews of rival pirate captains.

Britta raised her eyebrows. Illica, which had seemed so boring before, was suddenly sounding far more interesting. Avidly, she read on.

Illicans do not like to be reminded of their pirate ancestors. It is considered very bad manners to speak of them. Yet it is useful for traders to be aware of Illica's savage history, for it has given rise to many of the strange traditions that rule the lives of the islanders today.

When piracy began to be stamped out in the Silver Sea during the long reign of Deltora's first king, Adin, Illica was forced to change.

The last three pirate captains, still bitter enemies, retreated with their treasure to tall towers they built on the Illica hilltops in imitation of an older tower that had once existed there. From this time on, they denied the past and claimed to be merely wealthy collectors of fine objects.

In their absence, their crews made peace and gradually settled down to become fishing folk, farmers, boat builders and the like. As a result, a tidy town grew up on the harbor, replacing the clutter of filthy, rum-soaked shanties that had been there before.

As news of these changes spread over the Silver Sea, foreign ships began landing on Illica to make repairs and take on fresh supplies. The Collectors used these visits to find wealthy foreign brides, and to make it known that they were eager to trade for rare, precious items to add to their treasure stores. The hatred among the three was still intense, and the craving to outdo one another in the size and quality of their Collections had become the ruling passion of their lives. This fierce rivalry persists among the Collector clans to this day.

Fascinated, Britta flipped through more pages till another intriguing heading made her stop.

THE JAWS

In the early days of the pirate kings, a row of iron spikes was put in place across the harbor channel. This barrier, called "The Jaws," was made to lie harmlessly on the seabed until raised, by means of a great wheel, to block the channel and trap foreign ships trying to enter or leave the harbor.

"The Jaws" still exists today, though it is never talked about in public. By tradition, the people of the town keep the spikes and wheel in good order, but this is not discussed openly.

It seemed to Britta that there were a great many things in Illica that were not discussed openly. What a place! she thought. I will have to watch every word I say.

But on the whole, she felt very hopeful as she turned back to the first chapter and pulled out her notebook and pencil. From what she had read so far, one thing was very clear. The strange people of the towers were obsessed with their Collections. If they were offered something that would be the crowning glory of any treasure hoard—something like a rare sunrise pearl, for example—they would certainly do all they could to gain it. The fact that Britta had no proof that she had come by the pearl honestly would not worry the Collectors of Illica as it would worry the Rosalyn Trust Committee.

So with luck I will be able to trade the pearl for something of great value to carry back to Del, Britta thought. And then—then I will win the contest! I will become the Rosalyn Apprentice, and Mab's heir. I will win back the *Star of Deltora!*

She held her breath and listened for a moment to the soft creaking of the ship. It seemed to her that the *Star* had felt her thoughts, and was glad.

Then she put all such fancies aside, and set to work. She began reading intently, scribbling a note when she came across something of special importance.

She sighed, looking down at her shabby clothes, as she learned that Illicans still prized bright colors and fine garments as highly as their pirate ancestors had done. She raised her eyebrows as she read that the ruins of the first tower ever built on Illica were called the "Blind Tower" and thought to be haunted. She was relieved to find that she would be able to speak to the Collectors, and some of the townspeople too, in her own language. She smiled wryly at the warning that the Collectors traded only in precious goods, and would be gravely insulted if asked to pay for items in common gold.

Totally absorbed, she forgot about what she had seen and heard in the hold, forgot about Crow, forgot about the mysteries of Two Moons, forgot about her father …

The hours flew by. The dinner gong sounded, but Britta ignored it. She worked on steadily in a warm pool of lantern light, too intent on her newly discovered treasure to feel hungry or to wonder what time it was.

She did not notice the ship beginning to creak more loudly as the wind increased and the waves became larger. Tucked away in the cocoon of the reading room, her mind fixed on Illica, she failed to hear the first rumbles of thunder, did not see the first jagged streaks of lightning forking into the sea on the dark horizon ahead.

And she did not hear the wraiths that followed her everywhere moving uneasily in the deepening shadows, whispering of danger.

4 - The List

It was late when at last Britta threw down her pencil. Rubbing her eyes, she yawned and arched her back, stretching her cramped muscles. Then she jumped violently as she saw Jewel of Broome sitting at the other end of the table, powerful brown arms folded, bare, painted skull gleaming in the lantern light.

"Jewel!" Britta cried. "How long have you been there?"

"Quite a time," Jewel said lazily. "I wondered how long it would take for you to notice me. What is that you are working on so feverishly, all by yourself?"

Britta felt herself blushing as hotly as if she herself had hidden the Illica book away. "This book ... it is all about Illica! I found it—earlier today. You can have it after me, Jewel. I was going to tell you about it—"

Jewel laughed. "Oh yes, I am sure you were," she jeered, getting to her feet.

"I *was!*" Britta insisted. "Jewel, I swear!"

"Well, we will not argue about it," Jewel said. "I will leave you to your work. I tracked you down because I wanted to tell you that I have moved into Sky's old cabin. There is no point in the two of us sharing while the cabin next door is empty."

"Oh—of course," said Britta blankly.

Jewel shrugged. "Well, I am for bed, to get some rest while I can. A storm is brewing—a bad one by the smell of it—and I doubt there will be much sleep for any of us later. Good night."

"Good night," Britta echoed.

Jewel left, closing the door softly behind her. Britta sat with her hands clasped on the table, filled with a strange sense of loss.

She had not wanted to share a cabin at first, and she knew that it would be easier for her to keep her secrets if she did not have to do it any longer. As it was, Jewel had seen the goozli several times, though since it froze instantly the moment she came in, she thought it was just one of the little clay ornaments that were sold everywhere in Two Moons. But Britta had grown used to Jewel's cheerful company, and knew she would miss it.

She felt the deck tilting a little beneath her feet. The sea was restless. She should follow Jewel's example and snatch a few hours' sleep before the storm broke.

Something crackled as she pushed her notebook and pencil into her pocket. Wondering what it was, she felt for it and pulled out a crumpled slip of paper.

It was the receipt she had found tucked into the back of *Cladda's Mysteries of the Silver Sea*, the old book of legends her father had bought in Two Moons. She had pushed the receipt into the pocket of her second-best skirt and forgotten all about it. Well, she would dispose of it in the morning.

She smoothed out the receipt, meaning to fold it small and flat so that it would fit into her pocket more neatly. But as she made the first fold she noticed something that made her stare.

There was writing on the back of the receipt. It seemed to be some sort of list. Britta unfolded the paper again and examined the faded pencil marks.

127—

* Body of a turtle
* Where the sun could not find him (no windows—BT?)
* Cage of iron
* Shell of stone
* Wild sea
* "Return"

+ History

=???!!!

Thunder rumbled around the ship, but Britta

paid no attention. The words were in her father's writing. What did they mean? And why had her father used the back of the receipt to jot them down?

Because the receipt was in the package with the book, her logic told her. Larsett must have opened the package and started reading the moment he was alone. He must have been so excited by something he read that he began scribbling notes on the nearest scrap of paper—the back of the receipt.

What had he found?

Wincing, Britta glanced up at the dark shelf where *Cladda's Mysteries* lay hidden. She had resolved not to look at the book again. But she could not help herself. The number at the top of the list was a page number—she was sure of it.

In moments she was standing on a chair, feeling anxiously for the book. Once before she had found it missing—almost certainly taken away by Sky—but tonight it was there.

Without even getting down from the chair, she leafed through the book till she found page 127. Her knees went weak as she saw that it was the last page of the chapter called *Tier—the "Hungry Isle."* It described the final years of the pirate Bar-Enoch, who had taken the Staff of Tier from the dead hands of its creator and carried it away on his ship.

Britta's eyes burned as she began to read.

Bar-Enoch's reign of terror over the Silver Sea ended

when he, his ship, his treasure and the Staff of Tier vanished, never to be seen again.

⁘ It is believed that Bar-Enoch took the Staff into hiding, but his hiding place is unknown. The only clues come from strange tales told by members of the crew who deserted the *Serpent* in the year before it vanished.

Clues … strange tales told by members of the crew …

This was new. This was something that even the gossipy author of Britta's old favorite, *A Trader's Life,* had not known. *This* was why Larsett had been willing to pay such a high price for an old book in only fair condition! Clues to the whereabouts of the lost Staff of Tier!

Britta found that she was trembling, and quickly gripped the chair back for support. Gingerly she lowered herself till she was sitting safely, with her feet on the deck. She took a deep breath and read on, her heart thudding painfully every time she came upon a word or phrase that she remembered from the list.

⁘ According to the deserters' tales, Bar-Enoch had become obsessed with the fear that enemies were plotting to rob him of the Staff. Wary of everyone, he spent all his time alone and kept hold of the Staff night and day.

⁘ The legends of the Staff that Cures all Ills are many

and varied, but three things are common to them all. First, the Staff bonds to the name and the flesh of its Master. Second, on the isle where it was created, the wraiths it has enslaved will worship that flesh and that name as they worship the Staff itself. And third, the Staff will destroy any stranger who tries to claim it, even after its Master has grown tired of everlasting life, forgotten to take food, and died.

Bar-Enoch, then, should have felt quite safe. And so he did, for many years. But as time went on, and the Staff became the very reason for his existence, fears began to plague him. After all, he had found a way of defying the curse, so why should an enemy not do the same? What was more, he had taken the Staff away from the Isle of Tier, where it was most powerful, and left the wraiths to mourn its loss. These things preyed on his mind, no doubt, until at last he could think of nothing else.

As his madness grew, he was seen shaking his fist at the sun, cursing it for lighting the world and so making it easier for his enemies to find him. He was heard talking to himself in his cabin, mumbling of plans to crawl into the body of a turtle where the sun could not find him and where he would live forever, protected by a shell of stone, a cage of iron and the wild sea.

In his ravings he often used the word "return." His fearful crewmen were sure, therefore, that he was

planning to hide himself away on the haunted Isle of Tier, in the cavern where he had torn the Staff from the turtle man's dead hand so many years before.

⁘ But Bar-Enoch did not return to Tier. If he had done so, the Staff would certainly have caused him to make the island live again, to become the Hungry Isle once more, and this did not happen. So what did his strange words mean? Where was his final refuge?

⁘ It is most likely that the *Serpent* and the bones of her crew lie at the bottom of the sea, victims of Bar-Enoch's ruthless desire for secrecy about his hiding place. As for Bar-Enoch himself and the miraculous Staff ... their location remains a mystery.

Not to my father, Britta thought, glancing at the list on the back of the receipt. The clues in the deserters' tales meant something to him. He used them to find the Staff.

Shell of stone ... where the sun could not find him ... return ...

Britta snapped the book shut. An idea had come into her head that she did not want to believe—that she *refused* to believe. Clumsily she climbed up on the chair again and stuffed the shabby volume back into its hiding place. Then she pushed the chair back to the table and almost ran from the room, the receipt balled in her fist.

The little slip of paper had become hateful to her. She had to be rid of it—to be rid of it for good, and at once. Swiftly she threaded her way through the maze of dim, silent passageways, past the finalists' cabins and up the narrow stairs to the deck.

Only then did she remember the approaching storm. Wind beat in her face as she stumbled to the ship's side. A fishing net that had been hung over the rail to dry was flapping and wet with spray. The dark waves below were capped with foam. Lightning forked in the starless sky, followed instantly by a clap of thunder so loud that the rail shook beneath her hand.

It did not matter. What she had to do was the work of a moment, and she would be back in her cabin before the storm broke. She tore the receipt into small pieces, bent low over the rail and dropped the fragments into the sea.

She feared for a moment that the wind would blow them back to catch in the net, but it did not. Peering down, she saw the tiny scraps of white caught and swallowed by boiling foam.

Good, she thought fiercely. Good!

Then she screamed as her legs were jerked out from under her. And before she could think, before she could even scream again, she was over the rail and plunging headfirst towards the white-capped water.

5 - Peril

The attack had been too sudden, too unexpected, for Britta to try to save herself. The wraiths that moaned as they saw her fall were powerless to help her. Perhaps it was fate that had led her to lean over the rail just where the fishing net hung. Or perhaps she owed her life to young Davvie, who had draped the net over the rail, secured it so it would not blow away and then forgotten all about it. In any case, as she fell, the fingers of one of her flailing hands caught the edge of the rope mesh, and by instinct alone she held on.

She came to herself dangling helplessly above the churning sea, one arm stretched painfully above her head. The straining fingers laced in the net were already growing numb. Desperately she tried to twist her body, tried to catch the net with her other hand, but the wind and the waves were too strong for her.

She could do nothing but hold on, screaming for help, while above her the boiling sky cracked open and rain began to pound down upon her head.

Blinded by spray and rain, she did not see the figure peering down at her over the rail. Deafened by the thunder, she did not hear a voice shouting her name. The first inkling she had that help had come was a hand grasping her wrist, taking her weight.

Squinting up, she saw Sky bent double over the rail, his long hair whipping in the wind, one arm stretched down to her, the other reaching for the far side of the net.

"Britta!" Sky yelled. "Here! Catch hold!"

A fold of the net slapped across Britta's face. Feverishly she grabbed for it with her free hand, plunging her fingers through the rough, soaked mesh and clinging for her life.

She could hear Sky shouting again, but a fresh clap of thunder drowned his words. Then, suddenly, someone else was looming beside him. The next instant Britta and the net together were being hauled steadily up, away from the clawing waves and over the rail.

In moments she was lying on the pitching deck of the *Star*, unable to believe she was safe, and still fiercely gripping the net that was tangled around her. Panting and drenched, Sky knelt by her side, trying vainly to pry her fingers loose.

"A fine catch, Sky!" Britta heard Jewel roaring over the wind. "But, by the stars, you could have chosen better weather to go fishing. For pity's sake, let us get out of this! Move aside! I will carry her below net and all."

☆

Once they were out of the rain, Jewel acted with ruthless efficiency, bundling Britta into her cabin and sending Sky to the galley with orders to fetch a hot drink by fair means or foul.

Ten minutes later, despite the rolling of the ship, which made every movement awkward, Britta was huddled on the lower bunk, wearing her nightgown and wrapped in a blanket. Jewel was sitting at the writing table, glaring at her, when Sky came staggering back. He was carrying three tin mugs half-filled with steaming broth—filched, he announced with pride, from the pot always kept warm on the back of the stove for Mab.

"Britta says she did not fall overboard by accident," Jewel told him, after draining her mug in a single, angry gulp. "She says she was pushed."

"That does not surprise me." Sky sat down on the other chair and shook his head at Britta. "I told you to take care."

"You—" Britta's voice cracked. Her teeth would not stop chattering, and her throat felt raw. She took a sip of broth, winced as the warm liquid went down, and began again. "You are saying it was Crow?"

Sky shrugged. "Who else?"

When Britta was silent, he glanced at Jewel and raised his eyebrows.

"I believe Britta thinks it was Vashti—or else one of us," Jewel said. "It is hard to see why you or I would have pushed her overboard and then rushed to save her, but there it is."

"You were both there very quickly!" Britta burst out. "One of you might have been there all along, and—"

"By the serpent's fang, Britta, have you lost your senses?" Jewel cut in angrily.

Britta pulled the blanket more closely around her as if it were armor.

"I am sorry, Jewel," she made herself say. "I know that I would be dead now if it had not been for you and Sky. But someone aboard is my enemy. I was attacked in Del before the voyage even began. I was drugged in Two Moons. And tonight ..."

"Tonight was the work of Crow or one of his cronies, you can depend upon it," said Sky. "I would love to put the blame on Vashti, but somehow I cannot imagine her tipping anyone overboard. The worst Vashti has done tonight, I suspect, is to stay safely in her cabin, ignoring any screams for help she might have heard. Your enemy is Crow, Britta—I keep telling you. That mark on your forehead—"

"I had no mark on my forehead in Del—or when we first landed in Two Moons!" Britta broke in. "Crow had no reason to fear me then—he barely knew I existed! Why would he have wanted to stop me doing well in the contest? The only people who would have wanted that are … my rivals."

She lifted her chin and met Jewel's furious gaze and Sky's cold stare defiantly.

"Why, I had no idea you had the slightest suspicion of me!" growled Jewel. "You are far too closemouthed for your own good, Britta of Del! If you had spoken of this before, I would soon have put you right. Do you really think that a woman of Broome would dispose of a rival in order to win a contest? The very idea is an insult!"

"Indeed," Sky drawled. "And as I told you in Two Moons, Britta, even *I* have *some* standards. But you prefer not to believe that, it seems." He stood up, bracing himself against the table, and collected the empty mugs.

Britta bit her lip. She felt wretched.

"I *want* to believe it, Sky!" she exclaimed. "And I want to believe Jewel. It is just that … Oh, I am so confused! I do not know what to think, or who to trust!"

Jewel eyed her thoughtfully. Sky shrugged, and made for the door.

"Wait a moment, Sky!" Jewel said, her voice suddenly much calmer. "Let us put our pride aside and see if we can settle this once and for all. You and I cannot prove that we did not drug Britta, or try to push her overboard, but the first attack may be another matter."

Sky turned unwillingly and wedged himself into the corner of the cabin, the mugs dangling by their handles from one crooked finger.

Jewel looked back at Britta. "When exactly were you set upon that night in Del, Britta? Do you know?"

Britta nodded. "It was just past seven o'clock."

"As late as that? Well then!" Jewel leaned forward in her seat, her hands planted firmly on her knees. "At seven, I had made my trade and was walking down Anchor Street on my way back to the Traders' Hall. I heard the harbor clock strike as I reached the corner. And—"

"And you met me!" Sky exclaimed, lurching back to the table with the mugs clattering together in his hand. "Of course! We walked to the Traders' Hall together. We talked about whether they would feed us on our return."

"We did," Jewel agreed quietly. "And we were within each other's sight from that time on."

She sat back. "So, Britta, unless you think that either Sky or I can be in two places at once, you will have to accept that we are both innocent—of that attack, at least."

Britta could only nod. A wave of shame mingled with exquisite relief had flowed through her, warming her from head to toe. She looked from Jewel to Sky, and was thankful to see that they were both smiling.

"I—I am sorry for suspecting you," she managed to say at last. "It seems so foolish now. If only I had talked about this before! But I—I am used to keeping things to myself."

"So I have noticed," Jewel said dryly. "Oh, you and Sky are a deep pair—fine companions for a simple woman of Broome, I must say! Compared to you two, Vashti is as open as the day."

She saw Britta frown, and shook her head. "If you are thinking that it must have been Vashti who attacked you in Del, you should think again, little nodnap. As I recall, Vashti arrived at the Hall just after we did. I doubt she would have had time …"

"A street attack is hardly Vashti's style, in any case," Sky put in. "Hiding useful books so that no one else can find them is more like her."

"Do you mean the book on Illica?" Jewel asked with interest. "I thought Britta had hidden it!"

"And I thought *you* had, Sky," Britta exclaimed.

Sky raised his eyebrows mockingly. "I might well have done, if I had thought of it, but there was no need—it was already hidden when I saw it. I merely put it back where I found it—as we were told to do, you may recall. I found a few good books on Maris and Two Moons, as well, tucked away in unexpected spots."

He grinned at the shocked looks on his companions' faces. "It could have been one of Mab's little tests, but I would bet on Vashti. I think she bolted to the reading room and put the most useful books out of sight while the rest of us were settling into our cabins, that first morning. She was very out of breath when she finally joined us on deck."

"But we did not know which ports we would be visiting then," Britta objected.

"I suspect Vashti did," Sky said calmly. "Her father is powerful, and could well have made it his business to find out where the *Star* was to go. In fact, I would not be surprised if Master Loy had quietly bribed a Maris trader to give his darling daughter a very special bargain, to start her off well. Remember how angry Vashti was when the Keeper would not let us land? I have never seen her feathers so ruffled."

Jewel looked scandalized. "But surely no man of honor would do such a—"

"From what I have heard, Vashti's father would do almost anything to lay hands on the Rosalyn Fleet," said Sky. "In fact, I wonder ..." He looked at Britta thoughtfully.

"Great heavens!" Jewel exploded. "Are you suggesting that *he* attacked Britta in Del?"

"If he did, we will never prove it," Sky said slowly. "And in any case, it is not important anymore. Vashti's father is not on board this ship, but Crow is, and Crow is a far more dangerous enemy than Trader Loy, believe me."

Britta felt queasy, and again tightened the blanket around her shoulders.

"Crow can be dealt with easily enough," Jewel said impatiently. "When Britta tells Mab what he did tonight—"

"I cannot go to Mab!" Britta burst out. "Crow will simply deny he was the culprit, and we have no proof at all that he was. Besides, Mab is still angry with me for causing trouble in Two Moons. She is sure to think that I simply fell overboard, then claimed to have been pushed to cover up for my own foolishness."

"Or *imagined* you were pushed, which would be worse," Sky agreed.

Jewel glowered, but after a moment she sighed and shrugged.

"Have it your own way," she grumbled, getting up to deal with the fishing net, which was still lying in a sodden heap under the porthole beside Britta's clothes and boots. "But this secrecy is a mistake, you mark my words. Someone tried to drown you tonight, Britta. You cannot just forget it ever happened."

"There is no danger of that," Britta said, bending to pick up the torn white rag that had once been her second-best shirt and flapping it ruefully. "Just look at this! I read today that Illicans set great store by fine clothes. I now have the choice between this thing and the shirt that was soaked in mud at Two Moons. I doubt that either will make a very good impression on shore."

Jewel and Sky both laughed, and as this had been Britta's intention she laughed too. But beneath the laughter she was making herself a grim promise.

She would not report what had happened to her, but from now on she would follow Sky's advice. She would take care not to be alone, she would not wander the ship at night, and at all times she would be very, very wary. She knew her danger now. Crow would soon learn that it was not so easy to dispose of her.

6 - Helping Hands

In the days following the storm, Britta felt strangely peaceful. It was as if the terror of that night had broken the tension that had held her in its grip since Two Moons. Suddenly she felt alive again. Suddenly she could eat with relish instead of picking at her food, and sleep without being tormented by worrying dreams. When she walked on deck with Jewel she simply ignored the stares of the crew. Crow seemed to be keeping out of her way, because she barely saw him.

Much of her relief had to do with the new trust she had in Jewel and Sky. Without comment Jewel had moved back into the double cabin, plainly thinking that Britta needed protection at night. Britta was touched and grateful, though she felt fairly sure that no one would attack her below deck. A fall overboard that could look like an accident was one thing—a raid on her cabin was quite another.

The weather grew hot and sticky again. She and Jewel spent hours in the reading room together, sharing *A Trader's Guide to Illica* and talking about what they found.

"I have never heard of a land so strangled by tradition!" Jewel growled one afternoon, irritably tapping the open book with the end of her pencil. "Can you believe, for example, that the working folk still make offerings of food to the Collectors, just because their ancestors were fools enough to do it? You would think that by now they would be heartily sick of being looked down upon and ignored."

Frowning, she stabbed her finger at the lines that had offended her.

Neither the working people nor the Collectors ever refer to the "tribute" paid to the towers. The food is left at the tower doors by night and taken in at sunrise. This is yet another link in the chain that stretches back to the old pirate days when captains expected their crews to serve them without question. Foreign traders should always remember that personal contact is never made between the "noble" Collectors and the "common" people of the town.

Britta nodded. "I shudder to think how many blunders we might have made in Illica if we had not read this book before landing," she said. "It is such an odd place! The Collectors and the townspeople are bound together by all these secrets and customs, yet they live totally different lives. The only thing they seem to have in common is that they all love bright, beautiful clothing."

"Speaking of which ..." Jewel eyed her companion doubtfully. "Is that really the only shirt you have left, Britta?"

"Would I be wearing it otherwise?" Britta looked down at her shirt with distaste. She washed it every night, but it was still a dingy gray, and was looking more threadbare by the day. "I tried to mend the other, but it was hopeless. It was too badly torn and I am clumsy with a needle anyway."

Because I resisted all Mother's efforts to make me learn to sew neatly, like Margareth, she thought ruefully. I wish now that I had at least *tried* to do better.

"Vashti might lend you one of her shirts," Jewel suggested. "She says she will not be trading in Illica, so it will be no loss to her."

Britta shook her head. The thought of begging the scornful Vashti for a favor, let alone cramming herself into anything that had been close to Vashti's skin, was repellent.

Jewel shrugged and said no more, but the fact that she had spoken at all, when she herself cared so little for dress, made Britta realize just how shabby she must look.

She realized it even more forcibly that night

after dinner, when Healer Kay came to her cabin and handed her a roughly wrapped parcel.

"What is this, Kay?" Britta exclaimed, looking at the parcel in surprise.

"Mab sent it," the healer said, in her usual abrupt way. "The boy Davvie seemed unwilling to deliver it to you, so I brought it myself."

She glanced at the mark on Britta's forehead, ran her stubby fingers through her cropped gray hair, opened her mouth to say something more, then seemed to change her mind.

"Good night, then," she mumbled. She nodded briefly and stumped away, leaving Britta staring after her.

Inside the package was a folded length of multi-colored silk and a note:

Britta—I have no need of this fabric. Use it to make yourself a new shirt, for pity's sake. The one you are wearing is not fit to be seen in Illica.

Mab

Britta's face and neck grew painfully hot. She had noticed Mab, who had been present at dinner for once, giving her some sharp looks from the other end of the table, but she had not guessed the reason.

"Mab thinks that I will shame her in front of the Collectors," she said, showing the message to Jewel.

"Well, that is a stroke of luck for you," Jewel replied cheerfully. "This is very costly silk—though by the dust on the creases it has been folded away for quite a while."

She shook out the silk, which slid through her hands like a liquid rainbow. Britta stared at it greedily. Never had she seen anything so beautiful.

"Quite nice, is it not?" said Jewel, dumping the shining mass on the writing table and picking up her notebook. "Well, you had better get busy and make something of it. I will go next door and work there for a while."

"Wait, Jewel!" Britta wailed. "Stay and help me—"

Jewel laughed and made for the door. "Oh, no, little nodnap, you are on your own in this! I can stitch leather and mend canvas well enough, but I would not know what to do with a needle fine enough to sew silk like that."

When Jewel had gone, Britta took the goozli from her pocket and put it on the tabletop for courage and company. Then she fetched the sewing kit she had brought on the voyage in case a button came loose. She took out the tiny scissors that her mother had given her for her tenth birthday and hesitated, unwilling to cut into the beautiful silk.

The goozli put its head on one side and looked at her enquiringly.

"I have to make a garment of this silk, goozli," Britta said, feeling like a storybook princess whose task was to spin straw into gold. "Something I can wear in Illica—a shawl or a blouse, perhaps. But I do not know where to start!"

The goozli smiled, and held out its hand for the scissors.

☆

"By all the little fishes!" Jewel burst out, when she returned an hour or two later to find Britta sitting at the tidy writing table wearing a glorious new silk blouse. "You said you were clumsy with a needle, Britta! Why, the finest tailor in Del could not have done better! And how in the nine seas did you make it so quickly?"

"It was not difficult, as it turned out," Britta mumbled, with perfect truth. "But I fear I will not be wearing it in Illica."

She stood up and edged away from the table. Jewel's face fell.

The vivid colors of the blouse glowed against Britta's skin. The soft folds of silk crossed at the front and tied at the back, so there was no need for hooks or buttons. The blouse looked cool, expensive and elegant, and it suited Britta to a marvel.

It was perfect—except for one thing. It looked absurd with Britta's worn, sober, dull blue skirt. The garments seemed to snarl at each other like creatures from two different worlds.

"You see?" Britta sighed. "Not only do the colors clash horribly, but from the waist up I look like one person, and from the waist down I look like another!"

"Like a pig rat with a crest of parrot feathers," Jewel agreed tactlessly. She shook her patterned head. "What will you say to Mab?"

"I will only have to show her this!" Britta gestured hopelessly at her reflection in the mirror above the writing table. "One look will tell her that it is better to look shabby than ridiculous. But at least she will know I tried."

☆

And so it was that when, two days later, Britta stood on the deck of the *Star of Deltora* watching Illica grow larger on the horizon, she was wearing her usual hot, tight uniform of dingy white shirt, dowdy blue skirt and patched boots. Still, just in case the heat became truly unbearable, she had put the silk blouse into her shore bag, which she kept pressed between her feet to prevent anyone interfering with her water flask again.

The shore bag was really Healer Kay's. Kay had brought it to dinner one night and offered to lend it, having remembered that Britta had lost her own bag in the Two Moons swamp.

"You might as well have the use of it," Kay had said, waving away Britta's stammered thanks. "Mab is feeling poorly, so she and I will not be going ashore in Illica."

Thinking about that now, Britta shook her head. She did not quite know what to make of Healer Kay. Since the voyage began, Kay had seemed distant, as if her duty to Mab prevented her from thinking about anyone else. Yet in Del, before the *Star* sailed, she had proved to be an ally who could be depended upon in time of trouble. And the loan of the shore bag had been really kind and thoughtful.

Sky was also hard to understand. He was prickly and reckless, and thought nothing of being dishonest when it suited him. Yet he could be brave and gentle, and had his own sense of honor.

On a hurried visit to the double cabin the night before, he had dug a few silver coins from his pocket and put them on the writing table.

"You paid your last two golds for my life in Two Moons, as I recall, Britta," he had said. "Consider this a part payment of the debt."

"Oh, no, Sky!" Britta exclaimed. "You do not need to—"

"Take it!" Sky insisted, darting to the door. "Never fear—I came by it honestly. Mab has forbidden me to set foot on Illica—in her opinion I am no better than a stowaway—but I was given my shore leave pay anyway. Hara, at least, does not believe in slavery."

"Sky, why did you risk all this?" Jewel asked abruptly, before he could escape. "You must have known that you could not pretend to be female forever. You could not possibly have taken the Rosalyn Apprenticeship even if you won, so why enter the contest at all?"

Sky looked back over his shoulder and raised his eyebrows. "Why not?" he asked with a shrug. "I had nothing to lose and everything to gain. This voyage was a chance to see something of the world—perhaps to make my fortune, if luck was with me. I did not look further than that."

He smiled wryly as Jewel looked blank. "That is the simple truth, Jewel. I grew up on the banks of the River Broad, living by my wits. It was a hard school, and it taught me to take my chances where I found them."

Like my father in Del, before Mab took him under her wing, Britta thought now, remembering.

In the golden days before Dare Larsett left his family forever, he had often told Britta tales of his childhood on the streets—but only when her mother had not been there to frown and sigh. Maarie had preferred to forget that her husband had not always been respectable. She had also disliked being reminded that he owed everything to Mab, who had rescued him from the Shadowlands invasion, taught him to be a trader, given him a new life.

Britta bit her lip impatiently. Again, thoughts of her father had come to her just when they were least welcome. They had reminded her of something she had tried to forget. Like it or not, I am following in his footsteps, she thought, staring sightlessly at the island ahead. First Two Moons—and now this! Father must have visited Illica with Mab many times. He must have known it well. And perhaps, on his last voyage …

An image of the list on the back of the receipt floated into her mind, the words burning there as clearly as if she had never torn the paper to shreds, never seen it sinking beneath the foam. She gripped the rail. The shadows she had come to dread had begun flickering in the corners of her eyes.

Oh no, not now! Britta groaned silently. Not now!

If Lean Alice, fortune-teller of Del, had been with Britta at that moment, she would have seen the gray wraiths twining around the girl's rigid body, straining towards the horizon. Thurl, leader of the Two Moons turtle people and heir to the sorcerer Tier's magic, would have seen the same and felt more.

But Alice and Thurl were far away, and Britta had only her own small experience to guide her. As far as Britta knew, the shadows were creations of her own mind, and the thought was terrible and frightening.

I must forget the cursed list, Britta told herself furiously. I must not think of Father! I must rid myself of this notion that I am doomed to follow in his footsteps! It is a dark imagining that is making me ill, and I cannot afford to be distracted now.

"Leave me be!" she hissed at the shadows through gritted teeth. And to her amazed relief they drew back.

She could control them, then, if she tried hard enough. It was only a matter of will. With all her might she thrust the lingering image of her father's list away and focused again on the island.

It was closer now. Now she could make out a curving wall of cliffs rising from a broad expanse of shallow, foaming water. At the top of the cliffs there was a shimmer of green, and the shapes of three towers could be seen silhouetted against the sky.

Three towers—three Collector clans eager to trade … Britta's stomach fluttered. Her fingers pressed against the pearl nestled at the bottom of her skirt pocket.

The sunrise pearl was hers by accident, perhaps. But she had suffered for it—she had almost drowned in the Two Moons swamp to gain it. Now she was about to have the chance to use it, to win her heart's desire.

7 - The Collectors

By the time Jewel joined Britta at the rail a little later, the pale, choppy water of the shallows looked perilously near. "Hara is cutting it fine," Jewel commented. "Still, I daresay he knows what he is doing."

Sure enough, the next moment Captain Hara was bellowing orders and the crew was jumping to obey. Then the *Star of Deltora* was changing course, making a wide arc around the island to reach the deeper water that lay in front of the harbor entrance.

Britta had read of the narrow gap in the cliffs that led to the island's harbor. It was only when she saw the gap with her own eyes, however, that she fully understood how perfect Illica must have been as a pirates' hideaway.

The long channel of dark, restless water was just wide enough to take a single ship. Sheer rock rose perilously close on both sides of the *Star* as she slid between them with Hara at the wheel. Mab, magnificently dressed for shore, stood stiffly at the prow, silent as a painted wooden figurehead. The air was thick with tension. No one spoke.

Britta looked forward, imagining the iron spikes of the Jaws rising from the rippling water of the channel, barring the way. Tipping her head back, she gazed up at the ragged clifftops and imagined jeering, capering figures pushing great boulders over the edge to smash down on the helpless ship trapped below. She imagined cauldrons tipping, and cascades of flaming oil turning the ship into an inferno.

The visions were so real that she shivered and quickly looked down again.

"No wonder Illica is not on everyone's regular trading route," Jewel murmured beside her. "We can only hope that this is worth the effort. If we reach land only to be turned away, as we were in Maris and almost were in Two Moons ..."

"We will not be turned away," Britta said firmly, eager to convince herself as well as Jewel. "From what we have read, the Collectors think of nothing but adding to their Collections. And the ordinary people of Illica are plain, sensible folk."

Jewel raised her eyebrows. "You mean they do not have a magic bone in their bodies and will not sense evil on the ship even if it is here?" she asked dryly. "Ah, what a comfort you are, little nodnap!"

A minute or two later, the ship reached the end of the channel. The crew cheered as the *Star* moved out of the shadows into a calm, sunlit harbor where another ship, a fine two-masted vessel, already lay at anchor. Britta's spirits rose.

Ahead were a pebbled beach, a wide, sturdy jetty, a boat builder's yard and the white buildings of a town. In the background, on gently rising land, a patchwork of fields glowed green, yellow and deep gold. High above the fields, the three towers jutted importantly into the sky, bright flags flapping in the breeze.

Vividly dressed people were gathering on the jetty and waving from the shore.

"They look happy enough to see us," Jewel muttered. "Still, the people of Two Moons did too, at first."

"It will be all right," Britta said confidently, but behind her back she crossed her fingers for luck. Mab, she noticed, was standing as rigidly still as ever. The old trader was gazing intently at the jetty, her face deeply furrowed.

Mab is no longer as strong as she was, Britta thought, as she had thought several times before. She should have chosen an Apprentice long ago. I wonder why she did not?

Then, looking at that ruler-straight back and the crest of bright red hair, Britta thought she had her answer. Perhaps Mab had felt that to appoint an heir was to admit that her powers were failing. Perhaps she was unwilling to face the fact that old age and death came to everyone, even to legendary leaders like herself.

"What is she looking for?" Jewel muttered.

"The Collectors," a husky voice said behind them. "It seems that if *they* trouble to come down to the jetty, our welcome is certain. I hear that they will be your hosts while we are in port, by the way, if all goes well."

Britta and Jewel spun round. Sky was there, grinning at them. "The crew will have to find a bed in a tavern or sleep on board," he went on. "You two and Vashti, being the well-bred young traders you are, will each be invited to stay in one of the towers. That is the custom on Illica, it seems … for a reason you will soon discover."

He chuckled at their puzzled expressions and moved quickly away before they could ask any questions.

"Provoking wretch!" Jewel snapped, glaring after him. "What reason could the Collectors have for inviting us to stay except to make trade with us easier? And what business does he have looking so pleased with himself, in any case? He has been confined to the ship."

"He is in suspiciously high spirits, certainly," Britta said slowly. "I wonder—"

She fell silent as she saw Mab stalking towards them with Vashti trotting beside her. Vashti looked annoyingly trim and pretty in her crisp white shirt and demure blue skirt. Her eyes flicked over Britta and her small mouth curved in a smug, pitying smile.

"The Collectors have arrived to greet us," Mab announced curtly. "I should warn you that one or all of you will be invited to stay in a tower during our visit. It is the custom for such invitations to be accepted."

She glanced severely at Jewel, who had been unable to hold back a soft groan. "As I hope you know from your reading, traditions are all-important in Illica. Please remember that you are representing the Rosalyn fleet and behave accordingly. I want no trouble here."

She did not look at Britta as she rapped out that last sentence, but Britta knew the warning was meant for her, and her face warmed.

"Will *you* be sleeping in a tower, Mab?" Jewel asked with a touch of impudence.

Mab's lips twitched as if she was tempted to smile. "I will not," she replied. "It has been many years since a Collector has invited me to stay. There are few good things about growing old, but that is one of them. Please prepare for landing. I wish you good luck and good trading."

She turned on her heel and strode away to join Captain Hara at the prow.

☆

As the *Star of Deltora* docked at the jetty, most of the crowd melted away, respectfully leaving the Collectors to greet the visitors. The three haughty, gorgeously dressed people—two bearded men and a silver-haired woman—stood very obviously ignoring one another as ropes were tied and the gangplank lowered.

Britta's heart sank. Fervently she hoped that she would not be invited to stay in one of the towers. The working people of Illica looked pleasant enough, but these Collectors seemed another breed entirely.

Still, she reminded herself, Illica was the *Star*'s last port before the return to Del. And however sour the Collectors looked, they were the only people on the island who could afford to trade for a sunrise pearl. Her chance of winning the contest rested with them.

Unconsciously she smoothed her hair and began tucking her shirt more firmly into the waistband of her skirt. When she realized what she was doing, she almost laughed. It was as if she were armoring herself for a battle—a battle that could only be won by good grooming!

She glanced at Jewel, tall and straight, her shaved head decorated with swirling red patterns, her beaten metal armband and earrings gleaming. Jewel was completely relaxed. No one's opinion of her appearance troubled her.

Walking down the gangplank behind Mab, Vashti and Jewel, Britta felt eyes burning on the back of her neck. She glanced round. The sturdy, freckled young Illican woman who had deftly caught and secured one of the landing ropes was still standing at the edge of the jetty, watching the newcomers intently. Meeting her eyes, Britta smiled. The girl smiled back very briefly, showing even white teeth, then looked away.

The Collectors smiled too, when the travelers reached them, but the smiles did not reach their eyes. They were all middle-aged. The men's beards were fussily oiled and braided. The woman's hair was so stiffly arranged that it looked like a silver helmet. It seemed to Britta that a strange smell hung around them all. It was not exactly unpleasant, but for some reason it made her think of medicine and closed, stuffy rooms.

"Greetings, Madam Bell-Slink, Master Traki-Fen and Master Olla-Scollbow," Mab said with a slight bow. "How good it is to see you again after so long! May I introduce three young traders for whom I have great hopes—Vashti and Britta of Del, and Jewel of Broome. Vashti tells me she will not be trading in Illica, but Britta and Jewel hope to do so, I believe."

Britta writhed inwardly as three pairs of eyes scanned her worn garments before passing quickly on to Vashti and Jewel.

"Vashti!" Madam Bell-Slink exclaimed. "Why, bless me, if I remember rightly that is the name of the eldest daughter of Irma and Loy of Del! Can this charming young lady be she?"

Vashti dimpled at her. "Indeed, Madam Bell-Slink," she said. "My parents have not been able to visit Illica lately—they have so many business affairs to deal with at home nowadays! But they would be honored to know you remember them."

"Vashti, my dear child!" Master Traki-Fen cried,

stepping quickly forward and taking Vashti's arm. "This is wonderful! I know your father *very* well. Why, we were like brothers in the old days!"

"How strange!" Madam Bell-Slink said icily, her heavily ringed fingers closing on Vashti's other arm. "I do not recall that you were so very close to Loy of Del, Traki-Fen."

"Nor do I, I must confess," Olla-Scollbow drawled.

Traki-Fen smiled. "Ah well, our memories often fail us as we grow older, do they not? Vashti, my dear, I insist you stay at Fen Tower while you are here. After all, you are practically a member of the family! My wife and son would never forgive me if I let you go anywhere else."

"Oh, but Slink Tower would be far more comfortable for you, Vashti," Madam Bell-Slink said in a high voice, squeezing Vashti's arm. "My daughter is just your age, and my son only a little older. They have heard stories of your dear parents since their earliest childhood, and will be in a fever to meet you."

She tried to pull Vashti away from Traki-Fen. He hung on. Vashti's confusion was comical. She did not want to insult either of the Collectors, but if she did not decide between them quickly she was in danger of being torn in two!

Olla-Scollbow gave a short, sneering laugh. "How eager you are, my friends! Like a pair of dogs fighting over a bone!"

Mab, who had been watching the scene with

grim amusement, suddenly seemed to grow tired of it.

"I think, Vashti, that as Master Traki-Fen was the first to ask you to stay, it would be only polite to accept *his* invitation," she said.

"Oh, indeed," Vashti squeaked gratefully. "If you say so, Mab."

Madam Bell-Slink looked furious, but clearly knew when she was beaten. Grudgingly she released Vashti's arm, looked Britta up and down once more and turned to Jewel.

"I cannot take my eyes off your bracelet, my dear," she said, gesturing at the band clasped around Jewel's left arm, just above the elbow. "Forgive me for asking, but ... it is gold, I think?"

Britta was surprised. She would not have expected a Collector of Illica to mistake bronze for gold, however alike the colors were.

Then, to her astonishment, she saw that Jewel was nodding warily.

So I am the one who has been mistaken, Britta thought in grim amusement. It had simply never occurred to her that Jewel could own anything of real value, so she had failed to see the armband for what it was. She remembered taking Jewel for a deckhand when they first met, and wondered when she would learn not to judge by appearances.

"It is *most* unusual," gushed Madam Bell-Slink. "I would love to know how you came by it."

"I was given it on my fourteenth birthday, as is

the tradition in my family," Jewel said, a little stiffly but with perfect courtesy. "My brothers all have one like it."

"*Indeed!*" The Collector clapped her hands softly and darted a sly, triumphant look at Master Traki-Fen. "A gold armband for every child! What a *fascinating* tradition! And you have earrings to match, I see!"

She wasted no time after that in inviting Jewel to stay at Slink Tower in Vashti's place. She must have realized that Jewel would not trade the gold armband for anything she could offer, but she seemed not to care.

Britta was just wryly congratulating herself on looking too shabby to receive an invitation she did not want, when Olla-Scollbow turned to Mab.

"If you permit it, Trader Rosalyn, my wife and I would be delighted to offer our hospitality to the third young lady," he said, far more loudly than necessary. "The timing is perfect, because of course Scollbow Tower is the scene of great celebration just now."

"Indeed?" Mab smiled faintly.

"Oh, yes," Olla-Scollbow said, stroking his beard and glancing smugly at the other two Collectors. "My son Collin is to be married, you know—tomorrow, as a matter of fact—to a *very* charming girl from the Isle of Jade. Perhaps you have noticed her parents' ship anchored in the bay?"

"The Isle of Jade?" Mab raised her eyebrows. "My congratulations!"

"Thank you." Olla-Scollbow bowed, and again stole a glance at his rival Collectors, who were both looking as if they had just taken a bite from the same sour lemon. "It is quite wonderful to know that the Scollbow Collection will prosper through a new generation. And—of course—to know that my dear son has found happiness."

"Of course," Mab said dryly.

And suddenly Britta understood. Suddenly she saw the meaning of Sky's teasing remarks. Suddenly she realized why Collectors Traki-Fen and Bell-Slink had competed so furiously for Vashti, though Vashti did not intend to trade in Illica. And why Madam Bell-Slink had snapped up Jewel on hearing that Jewel's family was rich enough to give a gold armband to every child. It was not a matter of trade at all!

A huge bubble of laughter rose in Britta's chest as she recalled some words from *A Trader's Guide to Illica*. She had paid little attention to them at the time, but now they came back to her vividly:

As members of Collector families live in isolation both from the people of the town and from rival towers, they must find foreigners to marry. Ideally, though this is never admitted openly, the foreign brides and grooms bring riches with them, so that the Collections can grow.

Master Traki-Fen and Madam Bell-Slink wanted Vashti and Jewel not as trading partners, but as brides for their sons!

8 - Suli the Needle

Britta's urge to laugh was agonizing. Her eyes were watering, her chest was aching and she knew her face must be bright red. Desperately she pulled out her handkerchief, pressed it hard to her nose and mouth and turned aside as if she was about to sneeze.

"I hope she does not have anything catching," Olla-Scollbow murmured uneasily. "My son—"

"It is nothing catching, I assure you," said Mab, her steely voice showing clearly that she knew exactly what was ailing Britta. "Britta, we will excuse you if you leave us now. You and Jewel have some errands in the town, I believe?"

"Yes, Mab," Britta managed to say in a strangled voice. She noticed Jewel eyeing her curiously and snorted helplessly into her handkerchief.

"Off you go, then, the two of you!" snapped Mab.

"Your hosts will not be expecting you until sunset, I am sure."

"Quite! Quite!" said Olla-Scollbow hastily.

Bobbing an awkward curtsey to the Collectors, her handkerchief still pressed to her mouth, Britta bolted from the jetty. Almost choking, she hurled herself into hiding behind the nearest building and gave way to a perfect storm of laughter.

Jewel found her leaning weakly against the white wall, wiping her eyes, while the blue-clad workers in the boat building yard watched with interest.

"What is the matter with you?" Jewel hissed.

Britta gestured helplessly, appalled by her own behavior. What must Mab think of her? Let alone … She glanced towards the boatyard and saw that one of the staring workers was the freckled girl who had smiled at her on the jetty.

Sobered, she took a deep breath and began trying to explain herself. Yet, despite everything, as she confessed her fears that Madam Bell-Slink was hoping to secure Jewel as a daughter-in-law, her voice began to wobble dangerously. And one look at the horror on Jewel's face was enough to bring on a fresh gale of laughter.

"Stop laughing!" Jewel cried angrily as Britta bent double, clutching her stomach. "Imagine how it will be for me in Slink Tower tonight, with Madam parading her dear boy in front of me every moment! She might well refuse to trade with me when I reject him. By the heavens, Britta, you could at least show some sympathy!"

"I—I am sorry." Recovering a little, Britta mopped her eyes with her sodden handkerchief. "But it is your own fault, Jewel, for looking splendid and wearing a gold armband. No one wanted *me* as a daughter-in-law. Olla-Scollbow asked me to stay only because his son already has a bride and he wanted to boast about it to the others."

Snorting in disgust, Jewel set off along the street so that Britta had to run to catch up with her. It was not in Jewel's nature to sulk, however, and the boatyard was barely behind them when she gave a short bark of laughter. Britta looked at her in relief.

"I was just wondering," Jewel said, smirking, "how Vashti will get on with Traki-Fen's son."

Britta grinned and they went on with lighter hearts, the tiny pebbles of the road crunching beneath their feet.

In moments they had reached a busier part of the town. Here square white buildings lined the street, hiding the harbor from sight and blocking the faint sea breeze that had cooled the jetty. The air shimmered with heat. People smiled at the strangers as they passed by, many nodding in friendly greeting.

The buildings were shops and businesses, it seemed, though they looked like no shops Britta had ever seen. The white walls were clean and bare. All the doors were closed and shutters covered every window, no doubt to keep out the heat of the midday sun. The only splashes of color to be seen were the beautifully painted wooden panels that hung above the doors. The panels were all the same size, but each bore a different picture.

After a minute spent watching people bustling in and out of the shops, Britta realized that the pictures were signs—signs without words. A painting of a chair and a hammer meant a carpenter's shop. A steaming bowl and a spoon meant a place to eat. A loaf of bread meant a bakery.

Britta was delighted by the system. Jewel thought it was not very practical. "What single object painted on a sign could stand for a grocery shop?" she argued. "How could you tell whether a hammer and nails meant a carpenter's place, or a shop that sold tools?"

"No doubt the islanders know exactly what every sign means," Britta retorted. "It is probably a matter of tradition."

There the discussion ended, for a moment later they saw a sign that could not be mistaken—a dashing picture of a steaming metal tub with a striped towel folded over its side.

"A bathhouse!" they exclaimed together, and joyfully darted through the door.

A small man clad all in white bustled from the depths of his steamy but exquisitely clean domain and grandly introduced himself as Perlo the Bath. Having prudently taken the foreigners' money in advance, he presented his wife, Minta the Bath, his daughter, Hattie the Bath, his daughter-in-law, Suzelle the Bath and his niece, Freya the Bath, who divided into pairs and led the slightly dazed travelers away.

An hour later, Britta and Jewel were back on the street, feeling wonderful after a long, luxurious soak in hot, scented water.

Jewel's smooth brown skin was gleaming, and the red patterns that decorated her skull were brighter, but otherwise she left the bathhouse looking much the same as she had when she went in.

Britta, however, looked very different. She had left her hair loose to dry, and its dark, sweet-smelling waves floated lightly around her shoulders as she walked. What was more, unable to bear the thought of trussing herself up in her tight shirt again, she had put on the blouse the goozli had made for her.

She had hesitated only a moment before thrusting the hated shirt into her shore bag and pulling out the gaudy silk. The new blouse looked ridiculous with her sober skirt, perhaps, but it was deliciously smooth and cool against her skin.

That is the important thing, she had told herself, stuffing her flannel petticoat into the bag for good measure. It does not matter what I look like.

Her mother would disagree, she knew. But her mother was far away.

Jewel, at least, heartily approved of the change. "So you have come to your senses and dressed for the heat," she said. "Why, I have never seen you look so comfortable!"

Another companion might have added that the vivid colors of the silk were very flattering to Britta's dark beauty, and exclaimed at the glory of the shining hair rippling down Britta's back. But such thoughts did not occur to the practical Jewel.

They occurred to other people, though. The shoppers on the street now stared at Britta in frank delight, though their eyes grew puzzled when they noticed the drab skirt.

At last an old woman stopped Britta and began gesturing at a nearby shop.

"*Halish!*" the woman said, nodding vigorously and pointing to the shop sign, which bore a picture of a threaded needle and a scrap of yellow fabric. "*Suli! Halish po ingesni!*"

She gave Britta a little push, as if urging her to enter the shop, and looked dismayed as Britta smiled and shook her head.

"*Se halish* no good!" she said vehemently, pointing at Britta's skirt. "Suli the Needle—very good!" Again she pushed Britta towards the shop door.

"Why not oblige her?" Jewel said, looking amused. "There is no harm in looking. I will meet you back here in a few minutes."

So Britta, unwilling to seem impolite yet knowing she had too little money to buy new clothes, smiled again at the woman and went through the shop door.

Inside, it was dim and pleasantly cool after the heat of the street. One wall was lined with shelves stacked with folded fabric. Another was studded with hooks on which hung clothes of all kinds. A long mirror stood to one side. Beside it, sorting through a box of buttons, sat a round, curly-haired woman in a flowing garment of brightest green—Suli the Needle, Britta assumed. The woman jumped up, beaming.

"Ah," she cried, hurrying to Britta's side and fingering the cloth of the vivid blouse. "Very good! Maris—long time ago! Eight year? Ten?"

She held up eight plump fingers, then ten, and looked enquiringly at Britta with bright, birdlike eyes.

Britta shrugged and shook her head. She had no idea when Mab had bought the silk.

"*Soffa!*" the dressmaker said firmly, tapping the sky-blue streaks in the silk. "*Soffa* dye—very good! No more now. No more long time."

Tearing her eyes from the blouse, she looked down at Britta's skirt and pursed her lips in distaste. The next moment she had bustled to the wall behind her and begun sorting through the garments hanging there.

"No, no," Britta cried. "Please do not trouble yourself. I cannot—"

Suli took no notice. She grunted with satisfaction as she found what she was looking for, and turned back flourishing a skirt that fell into graceful ruby-red folds between her chubby hands.

"Halish po ingesni!" she said, nodding happily. She turned Britta to face the long mirror and held the skirt up to Britta's waist to show how exactly it matched one of the colors in the silk blouse.

Britta stared at her reflection, and felt a moment of intense longing. Never had she seen herself looking like this—the way she had always wanted to look.

The skirt could have been made for her. It was narrow at the waist and wide at the flounced hem, which just brushed the tops of her boots. The rich red fabric was strong, but soft to touch. There were even two deep, slim, buttoned pockets, craftily placed low in each side seam so they would not bulge, and almost invisible amid the skirt's liquid folds.

The goozli would fit neatly into one, Britta thought, and everything else would go easily into the other.

Then she pulled herself together and gently pushed the skirt away. "I am sorry," she said. "It is beautiful—very good—but I cannot afford it, I am sure."

She tapped her pocket, then shook her head and spread out her hands, to make her meaning clear.

Suli the Needle pushed out her bottom lip and glowered at Britta's dull blue skirt as if the very sight of it gave her pain. Then she brightened, pointed at Britta's shore bag and raised her eyebrows so high that they vanished beneath the mass of curls falling over her forehead.

"Trade?" she suggested, shaping her lips around the foreign word with care. "You have trade? Yes?"

Five minutes later, Britta was leaving the shop wearing the ruby-red skirt. Her old skirt was stowed away in her shore bag. The goozli, her comb, her notebook and pencil, and the sunrise pearl, wrapped in her handkerchief, were safe in her pockets. She was elated, though a little ashamed of her bargain.

She had paid for the skirt with the last of Sky's silver, the snack packet of dried fruit she had been given on the ship, her flannel petticoat and her crumpled shirt. Suli had shown by signs that the many tiny buttons on the shirt would be useful. But what anyone in such a hot place would do with a flannel petticoat, Britta could not imagine!

"A strange trade, indeed," Jewel commented as they walked on, attracting many admiring glances from passersby.

"I feel as if I cheated her," Britta agreed ruefully, turning to wave to the dressmaker who was still nodding and smiling after them at the shop door. "But she insisted! She just could not bear the way I looked before. She chose this skirt for me, and she was determined I should have it."

"Then she got what she wanted, did she not?" Jewel replied cheerfully. "Money is not the only measure of a good bargain—different things matter to different people."

"Yes." Britta nodded, thinking of an old man

in Del who had happily given her a masterpiece in trade for a modest little lantern that he wanted more than anything else in the world. "But she was very generous, all the same."

As she spoke, a sharp movement to her right caught her eye. She turned and saw Crow the bosun standing outside a tavern with his henchman Bolt and some other members of the ship's crew. Crow was jerking his thumb at Britta and muttering darkly. Some of his companions were sneering. The others looked fearful.

"Crow does not seem to admire your fine new garments," Jewel said dryly.

Shadows flickered before Britta's eyes. And suddenly she knew without question that Sky had been right. It was Crow who had tried to tip her overboard on the night of the storm.

Did his companions know it? Perhaps. Perhaps to them Crow was a hero. With an effort she resisted touching the amber mark hidden beneath her bangs.

"It is too hot and crowded here, Jewel," she said in a low voice. "Let us get out of the town and see something of the countryside."

Jewel scowled at Crow, but made no comment. She merely nodded and turned up a side street that seemed to lead towards the hills.

They walked without speaking or pausing to look at the shops and homes they passed. Very soon they had left the streets and white buildings behind and were climbing a steep path that ran between two fields.

Out in the cooler, fresher air, away from Crow's malignant stare, Britta felt better. Her fears had begun to seem rather foolish. Yet still she jumped as Jewel abruptly stiffened, drawing a sharp, hissing breath.

"What is it?" Britta cried. "What do you see?"

Jewel pointed down towards the curving edge of the bay, where a shelf of rock dotted with small pools of water had been exposed by the falling tide.

A lonely figure was walking quickly along the rock shelf, glancing over its shoulder now and then, as if to make sure that no one was following. Even at this distance, there was no mistaking the pale-colored tunic, the loose trousers and the mane of long, dark hair.

It was Sky of Rithmere.

9 - Body of the Turtle

Jewel grinned at the look on Britta's face. "I do not see why you are surprised," she said. "We both thought Sky had something up his sleeve. And surely you know by now that being ordered to stay on board would only make him more determined to sneak away the moment he had the chance?"

"Of course," Britta muttered, frowning down at the moving white figure. "I thought he might be planning to go up into the hills to search for the place they call the Blind Tower. A haunted, forbidden ruin is just the sort of thing to attract Sky. But what is he doing down there?"

Jewel's grin broadened. "Looking for trouble, I would say."

"Looking for *something*, in any case," Britta said slowly. And abruptly the suspicion that had begun smoldering in her mind flared into certainty.

She turned off the path and began to run down towards the rocks, the flounce of her skirt swishing through the long grass.

Jewel sighed, and slowly followed. "Sky knows his own business best, I think, Britta!" she called. "He will not thank you for interfering. And, look! He has reached the harbor entrance now. He will soon be through the channel and safely out of sight."

Receiving no answer, and seeing that Britta had no intention of stopping, she clicked her tongue in annoyance and lengthened her stride.

"By the stars, why can you not just let Sky be?" she demanded, when she caught up with Britta at the rocks. "For all you know, he may have had enough of Crow's bullying and decided to leave the ship for good. He may be planning to hide in the cliffs on the other side of the island till we have sailed."

"Then he is a dead man!" Britta retorted, dodging a rock pool that lay in her way. "Those cliffs are sheer, and once the tide rises again—" She broke off, shaking her head impatiently. "No, Sky is reckless, but not stupid. He must have seen the danger this morning, just as we did."

"Of course," said Jewel. "But you are wrong about those cliffs, Britta. They are not as sheer as all that, and they are pocked with holes and crevices, some quite large and well above the high tide line."

Britta glanced at her companion and slowed a little. She had not seen any holes in the cliffs of Illica.

But then, she did not have Jewel's amazing eyesight. Many times at sea she had heard Jewel identify a high-flying bird that to everyone else was a mere speck in the blue. And, in truth, she had been more interested in the hulking shape of the island, and in the three towers, than in the cliffs.

"I did not notice," she said thoughtfully. "But Sky would have done, I am sure. His eyes are almost as sharp as yours, and if he knew what he was looking for ..."

She nodded to herself and then, to Jewel's great surprise, began walking faster than ever, her eyes fixed on the rock point ahead.

"Britta!" Jewel cried in exasperation. "Have you not been listening to me?"

"Sky is not running away for good, Jewel, I am certain of it!" Britta panted. "I do not believe he has any thought of leaving the *Star of Deltora*."

"Why?" Jewel demanded. "Because he did not say good-bye to us? But to go without a word is exactly what Sky *would* do!"

She saw Britta frown, and as if suddenly mindful of her companion's feelings, went on in rather gentler tones. "Sky is one who walks alone. I have met others like him. Such folk may grow ... fond of people with whom they spend a little time. But they always keep a part of themselves separate, and secret. And when there is something else they need or want they will go after it, without looking back."

"Of course!" Britta cried impatiently. "That is the whole point!"

Baffled, Jewel shook her head and said no more.

At last they reached the channel that linked the bay with the open sea. The cliff face rose sheer above them, and the narrow shelf of exposed rock ahead was wet. A vast iron wheel, only slightly streaked with rust, stood in their way. Its base was sunk into a great groove in the rock, and fixed to both sides of it were wooden poles, each long enough for four or five people to stand side by side.

"This must be the wheel that raised the Jaws, in the old days," Jewel said, instinctively lowering her voice. "What a brutal-looking thing! You would think the Illicans would have better ways to spend their time than tending to an ancient monstrosity like this. These days it has no earthly use."

"Perhaps they are not so sure of that," said Britta. "Remember whose blood runs in their veins."

Feeling a sudden chill, she edged past the wheel and with Jewel complaining behind her, moved as quickly as she could to the end of the grim passage.

It was a relief to come out of the shadows—a relief to escape the feeling of being hemmed in by the towering rock walls that had seen such savagery and grief. The open sea looked clean and clear. The breeze smelled deliciously fresh after the stillness of the closed-in harbor.

Picking their way along the rocks, the companions

rounded the headland and reached the side of the island they had seen from the ship. At first they could see nothing at all but brown cliffs rising like a wall from the sea. Then Britta gave a soft exclamation, and pointed.

Some distance from where they were standing, about a quarter of the way up the cliff face, there was a flutter of white. As they watched, the scrap of white disappeared, swallowed in the darkness of an oddly shaped hole in the rock.

"There!" Britta crowed softly. "A minute later, and we would have lost him!"

"I heartily wish we had," grumbled Jewel, but plainly her curiosity had been roused, for she followed without further complaint as Britta began edging along the cliff face.

The task was not as dangerous as it looked. The tide was now very low. Rows of long, deep ledges that the waves had carved across the lower part of the cliff had been exposed to the air, and were almost dry. The ledges were so close together that with care it was possible to use them like a crazy stepladder, climbing higher up the cliff face at the same time as moving along it.

And this Britta did, with Jewel sidling after her. Silently they edged along, and whenever Britta stepped up to a higher ledge, Jewel followed.

Progress was slow, all the same. By the time Britta stopped, staring up at a dark cavity just above her head, Jewel had begun to remind herself that soon the tide would be turning once more.

Following Britta's gaze, she too looked at the hole, which for her was at eye level. They had passed other gaps and cracks in the cliff face, but there was no doubt that this was the one that Sky had entered. It looked deep—deep enough to be a true cave. And the shape of the opening was right—high and rounded in the center, with a long, narrow oval at one end and a much smaller oval at the other.

"The cave mouth is shaped like a turtle," Jewel said lightly. "Head, shell and tail—do you see?"

Perhaps she had hoped to make Britta smile, but if so she was disappointed. Britta merely nodded in an absentminded way and began looking around her, plainly searching for a way to climb up to the cave. And suddenly it seemed to Jewel that shadows were gathering around the figure of her friend—flickering around the ruby-red skirt, swirling behind the vivid blouse and fluttering hair.

Jewel shivered all over, then shook herself like a Broome fishing dog ridding its coat of water after reaching shore. This was no time for foolish fancies. She raised her arms, grasped the bottom lip of the cave entrance and hoisted herself up. She looked down at the rusted stubs of iron that formed a line across the dark gap. Then she knelt, and held out her hand to Britta.

Gratefully Britta took the offered hand. The toes of her boots scrabbled on the cliff face as she was hauled up to the cave.

"Once there was a barred gate here," Jewel said softly, pointing to the line of rusty pegs at their feet.

"A cage of iron," Britta murmured. "Between the wild sea and the body of the turtle. In the old pirate days, long, long ago."

As Jewel stared at her, she shook her head, blinking into the darkness of the cave. "I doubt that anyone in Illica today knows this place exists. Sky guessed it was here. I had the same clues—more clues, in fact—but Sky was the one who worked it out."

She laughed shortly. "Not so surprising," she added, with a trace of bitterness. "After all, I am just a trader—or trying to be. Sky is the treasure hunter."

She turned and crept into the cave. Wondering, Jewel followed her.

A short, rocky tunnel led into a low chamber, which seemed completely empty. The farther they moved away from the entrance, the harder it was to see what was in front of them. There was no sign of Sky, and when they called his name they received only mocking echoes of their own voices in reply.

"He is not here," Jewel said. "I would have heard him breathing by now. There is nothing here—nothing human, in any case."

"Then where is he?" Britta muttered. "He certainly came in, and he cannot have left—we would have seen him."

Jewel groaned and began feeling around the cave walls. "My brothers and cousins can all follow scents, but I was too interested in the sea and trading to practice that art," she said. "Now I wish I had not been so lazy. Sky has been here, and that is all I can tell. There must be another way out, but I warn you, if we have not found it in five minutes, I am giving up. This place does not suit me. It is like being buried alive!"

Under cover of the darkness, Britta slipped the goozli from her pocket. "There must be another way out," she repeated softly. "We need to find it!"

She put the goozli on the ground and it darted away, vanishing into the shadows.

"Talking to yourself will not help, Britta," Jewel growled from her place by the wall. "Search the other side, will you? And watch your fingers! I heard a scuttling sound just now—there may be nipper crabs in here."

But Britta had taken only a step towards the other wall when she felt something tapping the toe of her boot. She jumped, then realized that the goozli was back. She peered down and just made out the small shape at her feet. It seemed to be jiggling with impatience.

Seeing that it had her attention, the goozli scuttled a little way towards the back of the cave, then stopped and looked over its shoulder to make sure she was following. Cautiously she crept after it, taking tiny steps, afraid to go too fast in case she trod on it in the darkness.

The goozli seemed to have no such fears. Plainly

frustrated by Britta's slow progress, it began darting recklessly backward and forward in front of her, beckoning urgently as if it could not wait to show her what it had found.

And what it had found, hidden behind a section of the roof that sloped steeply downward, was so entirely unexpected that Britta gasped aloud.

"What is it?" Jewel called urgently, her voice echoing off the cave walls. "Britta, are you all right? Where are you?"

"Thank you, goozli!" Britta whispered, and felt the little creature leap onto the flounce of her skirt, skitter nimbly up to her pocket, and dive inside.

"Here, Jewel!" she cried, buttoning the pocket quickly over the goozli's head. "Right at the back! Come and see, but take care! The roof is very low for part of the way."

Arms stretched out in front of her, Jewel fumbled her way forward, freely cursing Britta, Sky, the dark—and herself, for being such a fool as to be drawn in to such madness. The curses continued when she was forced to bend almost double to get under the low part of the roof.

But when she reached Britta at last, when cautiously she rose to her full height and saw what stretched away in front of her from a faintly glimmering opening in the back wall of the cave, the curses died in her throat.

"A stairway!" she hissed. "A long, straight stair

inside the cliff, cut into the living rock! How is it possible? By the heavens, Britta, where can it lead?"

"A shell of stone," said Britta. And she stepped through the opening onto the stairway, blessing the dimness that hid from Jewel the fact that she was trembling from head to foot.

10 - Shell of Stone

They climbed for what seemed a very long time, but Britta did not stop for breath, even at the broad landings they came upon now and again. Her mind was racing, and it simply did not occur to her that she needed rest.

"I cannot believe this!" Jewel muttered at the seventh landing. "Why, we must be a quarter of the way across the island by now. Just think of the labor involved in carving out this stairway! Think of the time it must have taken!"

No time at all, Britta found herself thinking. But she could not rouse herself to speak.

At the tenth landing, her feet stopped moving of their own accord. Her skin began to itch and tingle. The landing seemed to be echoing with whispers. She told herself to keep climbing, but her legs would not obey her. She leaned against the stairway wall and closed her eyes. The cold stone seemed to throb against her cheek.

She felt Jewel take her arm. "Stir yourself, little nodnap," she heard her friend say bracingly. "It will do you no good to rest here too long. The air is not wholesome."

And with a sense of relief, Britta allowed herself to be dragged from the landing and pulled slowly on.

By the time they reached the next landing, the faint light that had glimmered in the stairway from the beginning had grown stronger. And soon they felt warmth, smelled fresh air, and realized they were climbing towards the sun.

The thirteenth landing was flooded with light streaming down from an opening at the top of the last flight of steps. The steps were littered with clods of earth, chunks of worm-eaten wood, clumps of grass and wilting flowers that must have fallen from above not long ago. Shading their watering eyes, Jewel and Britta moved on eagerly.

When they reached the opening they found that it was still partly blocked by rotting boards that seemed to be the remains of a trapdoor. Britta climbed through the gap easily, but several more planks heavy with dirt and grass had to be pulled away before Jewel could shoulder her way out.

They stood in the sunshine squinting and blinking like creatures of the underground dazzled by the light of day. It was very warm, but a small sea breeze kissed their faces and stirred the soft waves of Britta's hair. The fragrant air was filled with the buzzing, clicking and chirping of insects busy among the drifts of wildflowers that covered the ground.

They were at the highest point of the island. Not far below were the three towers, each one set in its own neat square of brown pebbles. Below the towers spread the patchwork of fields. Below the fields was the town. And beyond the town was the deep-blue bay, protected by its wall of cliffs.

Dazed, Britta stared at the peaceful scene, then looked down at her feet. Much had changed on Illica since the days when every pirate in the Silver Sea, from the greatest to the least, thought of it as a refuge. But the sea was the same. The cliffs were the same. And below the surface, the ancient rock kept its secrets.

"What is this place?" Jewel muttered.

Britta gestured at a long, low wall of weathered stone that stood near them, almost hidden by lanky tufts of grass.

"The Blind Tower," she said softly. "The first tower on Illica—or all that remains of it. It looked blind because it had no windows and no doors to let in the sun. It was a huge shell of stone, and the only way into it was that stairway leading up from the sea."

"How do you know that?" Jewel demanded, gazing at her curiously. "*A Trader's Guide to Illica* did not mention—"

"I read of it in another book," said Britta. "Like Sky."

Shaking her head, Jewel scanned the pretty wilderness, frowning at the humps and hillocks that showed where other great stones had been overgrown.

"There is not much of it left," she commented at last. "I know the Blind Tower was in ruins by the time the present towers were built. But still ..."

"It is very likely that the first Collectors stole most of its stones and used them to build their own towers," Britta said.

Jewel looked grave. "I wonder that they dared to plunder the leavings of the ancient one who created that underground stairway," she muttered. "Disturbing a powerful spirit means risking a curse that can never be undone."

A great wave of misery rolled over Britta, clouding her eyes, blotting out the sun. "Some people think they can dare anything and get away with it," she heard herself say.

"That is true," Jewel agreed soberly. "And the first Collectors were pirate captains. No doubt they were so used to killing for gain that they thought nothing of robbing the dead."

She shivered. And at that moment, quite near, there was a high peal of laughter.

Jewel and Britta froze. But when another slightly deeper and plainly human chuckle joined the first, they relaxed and exchanged sheepish glances.

"Well, *that* is not a vengeful ghost, at least," Jewel whispered. "Can it be Sky?"

"It did not sound like him," Britta replied doubtfully, "but who else can it be? Illicans never come here."

"Unless Sky is laughing all by himself, using two voices, one other person is here, at least," Jewel hissed. "Let us find out the truth of it. We can always slip away again if need be, and no harm done."

If it *is* Sky, who can his companion be? Britta thought, as she and Jewel crept forward, guided by more sounds of merriment. The laughter sounded so easy, as if the two hidden people knew each other very well and were perfectly relaxed in each other's company.

Like Jantsy and me, Britta found herself thinking, and wondered uneasily why that memory had come into her head, and why it made her feel a little hollow inside.

Insects fell silent as the companions passed, but the chorus of clicking and chirping started up again the moment they had moved on. The laughter had faded away, but now Britta could hear murmuring voices. They seemed to be rising from behind a sprawling mound of pink and white daisies not far ahead. She could catch no actual words, but the conversation sounded serious—even sad. It was as if the laughter had never been.

Britta began to feel uncomfortable. What right had she and Jewel to pry into a meeting that was plainly intended to be private? And yet, like Jewel, she could not bear to turn back without solving the mystery—especially with memories of the cave and the stairway so fresh in her mind.

The stairway and all it meant ...

They reached the mound of daisies, found footholds on the tumble of stone blocks hidden beneath it, and peered cautiously over the top. And there, in a shaded hollow, sat two perfect strangers, their hands linked over the picnic basket that lay open between them.

Britta felt her cheeks grow hot. She and Jewel were spying on a pair of lovers!

The young man was thin and very pale. The daisies that had been threaded in his silky black hair made him look faintly ridiculous, and this, Britta thought, might have been the cause of the brief laughter. There was no sign of laughter on the boy's face now. In fact, he looked miserable.

His companion's tunic and trousers made a bright splash of blue in the hollow. A chain of daisies hung around her neck and she was playing aimlessly with a few more flowers that lay in her lap. Then she looked up, and with a little start, Britta recognized the square, freckled face of the Illican girl who had smiled at her on the jetty.

Suddenly terrified that she would be seen, Britta ducked her head and stepped back—a little too far. Her heel slipped off the block she was standing on, and daisy stems snapped like fireworks as she grabbed at them to save herself from falling.

There were cries of shock from the hollow. The next minute, some daisy stems were thrust aside and the young man's face, paler than ever, appeared in the gap.

Britta, frozen half on and half off the block of stone, began gabbling apologies. The boy goggled at her for a long moment, then abruptly slithered back into the hollow. There was a frantic muttering and scuffling, the sound of two pairs of running feet … then silence.

"Remind me never to take you hunting with me, Britta," Jewel said with a sigh, stepping down from her own perch. "You have no talent for hiding, I fear—unlike some." She raised her voice slightly. "Very well, Sky! You can show yourself now."

There was a rustle to their right as Sky stood up and edged out of the daisy tangle in which he had been crouching, totally concealed. His lips twitched at the look on Britta's face.

"I am grateful to you for scaring those two lovebirds away," he said, casually brushing away the petals that clung to his tunic. "I have been trapped here, afraid to move, ever since they arrived. If they had seen me, Mab might have heard of it. She has eyes and ears everywhere."

He put his hands in his pockets and regarded Britta with his head on one side. "So you have been shopping, Britta! You look very fine, I must say—quite fine enough to win the love of a Collector's son, if that was your intention."

"It certainly was not!" Britta snapped. "I—"

"Do not rise to his bait," Jewel cut in. "He is only trying to distract you."

She turned to Sky. "We followed you around the rocks," she said bluntly. "We found the cave and the stairway."

"Did you indeed?" Sky raised his eyebrows. "So my secret is out! Not that it matters now. For all my hopes, I found no sign of treasure down there—or up here either."

"Treasure?" Jewel echoed. "By the heavens, Sky, what made you think—?"

"The tenth landing," Britta found herself saying.

She hunched her shoulders as both her companions stared at her. "I had a—a feeling—on the stairway, as we reached the tenth landing from the bottom."

"A feeling," Sky repeated flatly.

Britta swallowed, and nodded. "I think there is something hidden there. There, or somewhere very near."

She did not know why she was suddenly so sure what the strange, troubling emotion that had seized her on the tenth landing had meant. She did not know if telling Sky and Jewel about it was wise or foolish. She only knew that she could not leave Illica without knowing the truth, and after today she might not have another chance to find it out.

She saw that Jewel looked dubious, Sky frankly amused. "Believe me or not, as you like!" she exclaimed, with a flash of temper. "I am going back down to look."

"I am not doubting you, Britta," Jewel said peaceably. "You have very good instincts when it comes to finding things. But that landing is a long way from the daylight. We will barely be able to see our hands in front of our faces down there, let alone find something meant to be secret."

Sky's face had changed while Jewel was speaking. His mocking grin had vanished. Now he looked eager. He tapped his pocket. "I have part of a candle left," he said. "Come on!"

And so it was that Britta, Sky and Jewel went back into the underground and slowly made their way down the stairway, counting the landings as they went. So it was that they moved from sunlight into dimness, and at last reached the fourth landing from the top.

Britta had not needed to count. A deep trembling had begun in the pit of her stomach the moment she set foot on the smooth, bare space. In front of her, the stairway continued down, dim and secret. Behind her, it stretched up to the sun. But the mystery was here—she knew it.

She tried to speak, but found she could not. She turned to her left, and put her hands to the shadowed rock wall.

It was Sky who found the knob of stone that opened the hidden door in the wall. Once the knob had been twisted, the great slab of rock swung inward beneath his hand as smoothly as if it had been oiled. A gust of stale, reeking air billowed out onto the landing as an echoing black cavern was revealed.

Jewel cursed under her breath. Sky made no sound, but his fingers shook as he struggled to light the candle. Britta waited, forcing herself to remain still, though her whole body was straining towards the darkness as if urgent, invisible fingers were pressing her forward.

"One of us should wait here," Jewel muttered, when the candle was alight. "That door is a sorcerer's trick. I do not trust it. For all we know it will swing shut the moment it feels feet cross its threshold, and seal the intruders inside."

Sky nodded in vague agreement, but plainly had no intention of being the one to stay behind. He plunged through the doorway, the candle held high. Britta appeared not to have heard Jewel at all, for she followed him without a backward glance.

Scowling, Jewel stayed where she was, peering after the candle flame as it grew smaller in the darkness.

So Sky and Britta shuffled alone through the dry sand that covered the cavern floor. They were alone when they reached the back wall of the place, and in silence, by the flickering candlelight, read the words engraved on the smooth surface:

I AM THE MIGHTY BAR-ENOCH, MASTER OF THE STAFF OF LIFE AND DEATH. INTRUDERS ON MY PEACE, DEPART! ENVIOUS THIEVES, BEWARE! BY THE MAGIC OF THE TURTLE MAN THE STAFF FIRST CAME TO ME. IT KNOWS MY FLESH. IT KNOWS MY NAME. IT CLEAVES TO ME ALONE. SHOULD I GROW WEARY OF THIS LIFE, MY DEATH WILL NOT DIVIDE US. ANY LIVING SOUL WHO TRIES TO TAKE IT FROM ME WILL BE SLAIN.

Sky lowered the candle.

Sitting propped against the wall beneath the engraved words was all that remained of the mighty pirate Bar-Enoch—a shriveled corpse with crooked, empty hands.

11 - In the Dark

Blackened skulls and crumbling bones lay half-buried in the sand around the dead man's feet. It seemed that Dare Larsett had not been the first to defy the warning on the wall. Many before him had tried to rob Bar-Enoch's body, so horribly preserved long after it should have fallen to dust. Larsett must have stepped over their bones to wrest the Staff from those clawlike hands and take it for himself.

Britta's throat closed. Shuddering, she turned her face away from the rag-clad husk and the boastful warning that seemed to mock it so cruelly. Her mind was suddenly teeming with whispers. They were the same ghostly, hissing voices that had plagued her since the voyage began, but here in this dreadful death chamber they were far stronger, far louder. She could not banish them. They were beyond her control, just as they had been in the *Star*'s cargo hold, when she had looked down at the iron box.

And she could hear what they were saying. She could hear every feverish, gloating word, and the name, repeated and repeated in gleeful triumph. *Larsett! Larsett! Larsett! …*

She clapped her hands to her ears, but nothing could shut the whispers out. Trapped in a nightmare of sound, feeling that her head would burst, she groaned aloud, swaying where she stood.

Sky caught her just before she fell. She felt his arms around her, heard him telling her that he was sorry, that he should have realized she had never seen a dead body before, that he should have warned her—

"No!" Britta moaned, hardly knowing what she was saying. "It is the voices! The voices! They are glad that Bar-Enoch's fears finally drove him out of his tower, made him bury himself in this ghastly hole. They are glad he let himself starve to death, glad he lies here alone, glad he was cheated of the Staff … Oh, I cannot bear it!"

And abruptly, her mind was free—blessedly empty of sound. Stunned, she realized that the moment she had spoken of the whispers, they had stopped.

Sky had become very still. "Voices?" he asked softly.

Britta's stomach turned over. How could she have betrayed herself? How could she have babbled of the whispering voices—to Sky, of all people! He would think she was sick in her mind like the old potter

Sheevers, like all those sad others who even the king of Deltora could not cure.

"What voices, Britta?" Sky persisted, a little more urgently.

Britta pulled away from him. Desperately she tried to cover up her mistake. "Oh, do not fear, Sky—I have not lost my wits!" she said, forcing a laugh. "This cavern would make anyone hear things, but I am quite myself again now."

Her voice sounded thin, and it was far higher than normal. She knew that Sky would not be deceived, and waited in dread for his reply.

When it came, it astounded her. Sky gave a low chuckle.

"You cannot fool me, Britta!" he said. "You have given yourself away at last. But by the stars, how closely you have kept your secret—as closely as I kept mine! Or … does Jewel know? Does Mab?"

"No," Britta murmured in confusion.

"Then they will not hear it from me, you can be sure of that."

There was no pity in Sky's voice. If anything, he sounded excited—more animated than Britta had ever heard him sound before.

"No wonder you are good at finding things," he went on eagerly. "Ah, just imagine being able to hear and see the memories stored in the walls of ancient places! It is a rare talent! I have read of it, but have never before met anyone who had it."

Britta stared blankly into the darkness as slowly his words sank in. She, too, had read of people who could "feel" memories locked in iron, stone, deep pools of water and ancient forests. It had not occurred to her that she might be such a one.

But if she was—if Sky was right—then she no longer had to doubt her sanity. Ever since she had entered the Trader Rosalyn contest she had been hearing things that other people did not hear, feeling things that other people did not feel. But perhaps the hope, fear and excitement of her quest had unlocked a gift she had always possessed without knowing it.

A great wave of relief rolled through her. She swung round to Sky and saw mingled fascination, respect and envy in the clever face lit by the wavering candle flame.

"What is happening in there?" Jewel roared from the entrance.

"We are quite safe, Jewel!" Sky shouted back. "Two minutes more and we will be with you!"

He bent and swept the candle's feeble light over the scuffed, sandy floor. Ruefully, he shook his head.

"I had hoped to find some small remains of Bar-Enoch's treasure here," he muttered. "He must have brought his best pieces with him when he retreated from his tower. No doubt this cavern once glittered like a dragon's hoard. But it has been picked clean. The early Collectors, I daresay, found this place and secretly took away anything they could lay their hands on."

"Except the Staff of Tier," Britta could not help saying.

"Except that," Sky said seriously. "After the first deaths, they left the Staff alone. So here it stayed, long after the stairway was forgotten and the entrance from the ruined tower overgrown. Then, just a few years ago, Dare Larsett came and broke the spell—how, I would give my right hand to know."

He paused, but when Britta said nothing he went on, plainly enjoying speaking of things he had been thinking about ever since finding the clues in the *Mysteries* book.

"No doubt Larsett had the *Star of Deltora* anchored far off shore, where it would not be seen. Then he rowed in to the turtle cave by night. That is what I would have done."

Again he paused expectantly. Knowing she had to make herself speak before her silence became too obvious, Britta swallowed.

"And he left the same way," she said. "So no one in Illica knew he had ever been here. And perhaps no one on the *Star of Deltora* knew either." She was gripped by a feeling of unreality. It was so strange to speak of her father like this—as if he were a stranger. But of course that was what he was to Sky.

"Some crew members must have known," said Sky. "Larsett must have had companions when he rowed in. No doubt it was their voices you heard, rejoicing because he had defied the curse and survived."

"Companions?" Britta repeated faintly. Somehow she had always imagined her father taking the Staff alone. She remembered the gale of gleeful whispers, and felt sick.

Sky nodded. "Larsett would have needed help to move what he had brought with him."

Again he lowered the candle. Amid the footprints in the sand, a deep channel showed that something heavy, with square corners, had once been dragged to the cavern doorway.

"There is a long, lead-lined box still bolted into the ship's cargo hold," said Sky.

"I know," Britta murmured. Her heart twisted in her chest as she remembered what she had seen and heard when she opened the box.

Memories, she told herself. Just memories held in the metal.

"Larsett no doubt thought that the lead would shield him from the power of the Staff," Sky went on. "But he was wrong. The Staff possessed him and made him take it to where it wanted to be—the heart of the Hungry Isle."

"You sound as if you are sorry for him!" Britta burst out.

Sky shrugged. "Perhaps I am, in a way. People call him evil now, but the same people admired him beyond all reason before his fall. He was warm and generous, by all reports, as well as being a superb trader. I think he was just a vain, reckless adventurer who was used to success and who one day dared too much."

Seeing Britta's blank stare and mistaking the reason for it, he gave a crooked grin. "Yes, I know! I have told myself many times that I must not make the same mistake."

He turned towards the cavern doorway, his hand curved around the candle flame. "There is no point in staying any longer. If there is anything of value left in this place, it is buried in the sand and lost."

"You go ahead," said Britta. "I will follow."

Sky glanced back at her quizzically, then gave a shrug and moved on.

Britta took the goozli from her pocket and whispered to it as she set it down. As it vanished into the dark she paced slowly after Sky, guided by the small dim light of the candle flame.

She had taken only a step or two before the goozli scuttled up to her, dropped some objects into her lowered hand and shot away again. It had returned to her twice more and was safely back in her pocket before she reached the cavern entrance.

Plainly Sky had wasted no time in reporting on what they had seen, for Jewel was cursing in disgust as Britta stepped out onto the landing. The curses changed to gasps of wonder as Britta held out her overflowing hands.

Sky gazed in silence at the collection of small treasures—two heavy old gold coins, a tangle of gold chain, a delicate jade bracelet and a woman's hair clip set with what looked like sapphire chips.

"These were in the sand, just as you said, Sky," said Britta, suddenly longing to be rid of objects that to her reeked of terror and bloodshed. "Take them."

Sky shook his head. "You found them. And you found the cavern, too. They are yours by right."

"They are not," Britta insisted. "I would never have known the cavern existed if Jewel and I had not followed you."

His eyes on the glimmer of the gold in her hands, Sky shook his head again and put his own hands behind his back.

"By the serpent's fang, you two will drive me wild!" Jewel exploded. "For pity's sake, close that death chamber and let us get back into the open air before I suffocate! As for that treasure, Britta, if Sky will not have it and you will not keep it, throw it back where it came from! I would not touch it for all the gold in the nine seas!"

She stormed on up the steps, without looking back.

Sky made a wry face. "Be cursed if I will let you throw those things away, Britta! I will take them, since you insist—all but one. You keep the hair clip, at least. It will suit you—now that you have stopped trying to look like a prim little trader's daughter at last."

Britta felt a sharp stab of anger. At first she did not quite understand why, then she knew. She had reacted to Sky's superior tone, the casual insult to what her poor mother had so wanted her to be.

"You know nothing about me, Sky!" she flashed back. "Perhaps you like my new clothes better than my old—well, so do I! But I have never *tried* to look like anything. I dress in what I have—as you do."

Thrusting the little hoard of treasure into Sky's hands, she almost ran up the stairs, leaving him staring after her.

☆

There was very little talk when the three companions met again above ground. As usual, Jewel's irritation had passed quickly, but she could feel the tension between Britta and Sky, and this kept her quiet. The moment the stairway opening had been covered once more, this time with stones, Sky set off for the ship, barely pausing to nod a casual farewell.

"We can only hope that he will be able to creep on board without being noticed," Jewel said lightly. "In the meantime, we had better make our way to our towers, Britta. The sun will soon be setting."

She led the way out of the ruins and down the hill. "It would be best to tell no one about finding that death chamber," she remarked after a few moments. "If the Collectors do not like their pirate ancestors to be mentioned, they certainly would not want to be reminded that their precious Collections include treasure robbed from Bar-Enoch's hoard."

Britta laughed shortly. "I doubt they know. It is likely that when the first Collectors discovered the hoard they kept the secret to themselves and spread the word that the Blind Tower ruins were haunted, to scare others away. It is also likely that once they had robbed the cavern they put it out of their minds and never spoke of it ever after, even to their families, so their secret died with them. You remember what we read of them!"

"Indeed." Jewel made a disgusted face. "They were determined to seem respectable. Respectable—hah! I wonder how many poor souls they forced to lay hold of the Staff of Tier, before deciding that the curse could not be broken?"

"Too many," Britta answered in a low voice, remembering the bones in the sand.

By now they were nearing Slink Tower, and Jewel groaned as she saw Madam Bell-Slink waiting by the door with a gangling, stoop-shouldered young man. At a sharp word from his mother, the young man straightened abruptly. Jewel groaned again.

"Have a pleasant evening," Britta said dryly. She skirted the pebbled square and walked on, leaving Jewel to her fate.

12 - Scollbow Tower

Scollbow Tower was the next in line, rising tall and stark against the reddening sky. As she trudged towards it, Britta forced the events of the afternoon out of her mind and concentrated instead on the all-important trade to come.

She had to think coolly and carefully about what Olla-Scollbow showed her, rather than jumping at the first enticing thing she saw. Perhaps he would try to hurry her, using the wedding as an excuse, but she must refuse to be hurried.

He would certainly ask what she had to trade, but she had already decided that she would not tell him at once. She would take her shore bag with her to the meeting, so he would not even know how large or small her trade item was.

She was determined not to show the sunrise pearl until she had seen what she wanted in exchange for it. If Olla-Scollbow had time to think, he might realize that without a receipt it would not be easy for Britta to trade the precious pearl anywhere else. He might keep his most valuable things back, hoping to secure the pearl cheaply. It would be best to take him by surprise.

Britta was thinking so intently that she was quite startled to find her boots crunching on pebbles and to see the door of the tower before her. She took a deep breath, lifted the heavy knocker and let it fall.

After a moment or two, the door swung open, and there was Olla-Scollbow, his pale, bulging eyes widening in surprise at the sight of his visitor's new clothes.

"Well, well!" he exclaimed, ushering her into a dim and echoing entrance hall where a small group of finely dressed people stood stiffly sipping drinks. "Here is our guest from the *Star of Deltora*—and what a *great* pleasure it is to see you, ah—my dear!"

Plainly he had forgotten Britta's name, but otherwise things were going well. Britta touched the sunrise pearl in her pocket. It would not be difficult to trade the pearl for something wonderful if Olla-Scollbow remained in his present good mood. Jewel would have to try to trade with her hosts while at the same time fending off a betrothal. For Britta, on the other hand, there were no awkward problems.

His chest swelling with pride, Olla-Scollbow drew forward a plump, rather sleepy-looking young woman who was encased in frilled pink satin and perfectly dripping with jewels.

"This is the queen of this evening, my adorable future daughter-in-law, Mishatweet of the Isle of Jade," he announced. "I first set eyes on her only a month ago, but already I love her like one of my own!"

Britta curtseyed. Mishatweet curtseyed in return, smiled vacantly and plucked at one of her frills.

"And this is my son, Collin," Master Scollbow went on, beckoning impatiently to someone on his left. "He is feeling a little shy tonight, it seems, but you must forgive him, my dear—ha, ha! After all, tomorrow is his wedding day!"

He dragged his son into Britta's line of vision. And Britta found herself looking into the horrified eyes of the pale young man she had last seen holding hands with the freckle-faced girl in the ruins of the Blind Tower.

She stifled a gasp of shock and inwardly cursed her bad luck. Just when she was thinking that she would have an easy time of it in Scollbow Tower, here was a complication that could ruin everything!

But only if she lost her head, she told herself. Keeping this firmly in mind, she pulled herself together and managed to nod politely to Collin as if she had never seen him before.

His eyes, which had been fixed beseechingly on hers, glowed with relief, and at once she was filled with contempt. Collin had looked on the freckled girl with love—that was certain. Yet he was to marry another young woman tomorrow! What sort of man was he?

A trace of what she felt must have shown on her face despite all her efforts, because Collin blinked as if he had been slapped before hurriedly turning away.

Luckily, Olla-Scollbow had noticed nothing. Grandly he led Britta on to meet Mishatweet's parents, who were both very stout and looked stifled in their rich clothes. Mishatweet's mother wore even more jewelry than her daughter, and a tall, fluffy feather fixed to a circlet of jade bobbed above her head, often tickling her husband's nose.

Despite their obvious wealth, the two were clearly very much in awe of Olla-Scollbow. They bowed to Britta with great respect as Olla-Scollbow introduced her as "the Rosalyn fleet's most promising young trader," with whom he must do business first thing in the morning.

The woman murmured that it was a pity their host had to work on his son's wedding day.

"Ah, well!" Olla-Scollbow sighed and rolled his eyes. "There is no rest for a Collector of Illica, I fear, dear lady. Business comes first—my position demands it."

Pompous old goat, Britta thought, as the couple exclaimed in nervous sympathy. Mindful of the next day's trading, however, she kept smiling as she was borne off to meet Olla-Scollbow's thin, bitter-looking wife, Lady Poltice, who was very grand in purple silk and elbow-length black lace gloves.

"Thank you for having me to stay, Lady Poltice," Britta murmured, as the woman's sharp little eyes flicked up and down, taking in every detail of her new guest's appearance.

"A pleasure, I assure you," Lady Poltice replied coldly, and shot her husband a sour glance that made her true feelings very clear.

Looking a little flustered, Olla-Scollbow turned his back and made a great show of pouring wine into a huge silver goblet. He gave the goblet to Britta then hastily excused himself and bustled back to Mishatweet's parents with the wine jug. Left alone with her silent hostess, Britta tilted the goblet to drink and found that it contained no more than a teaspoon of watery liquid. Olla-Scollbow must have been even more flustered than she had thought. She took a tiny sip and racked her brains for something to say.

"What a beautiful goblet!" she said desperately at last.

"Of course," Lady Poltice said, raising her thin eyebrows and smoothing her gloves. "It is part of the Collection."

At that moment, a pale young girl in a heavily beaded velvet dress appeared at Britta's side, shyly holding out a crystal bowl half-filled with salted nuts. Britta's mouth watered. She had eaten nothing since breakfast, and the sight of food made her realize how hungry she was.

Smiling her thanks she reached into the bowl, but

before she could take a single nut Lady Poltice amazed her by seizing her wrist and pulling her hand back.

Startled in more ways than one, Britta looked round at the woman, her eyes wide.

Lady Poltice gave a high, false laugh, dropped her guest's wrist as if it had scalded her, and smoothed her gloves again.

"Poupette, what are you thinking of?" she scolded. "Our guest does not want to spoil her appetite at this late hour, when dinner is about to be served! Take those nuts back where they belong!"

The girl in velvet flushed painfully. "Yes, Mama," she squeaked, and scuttled off, almost tripping over her heavy skirts in her haste.

A little gust of the medicine-like smell that seemed to surround all the Collectors wafted into Britta's nostrils, and suddenly she realized why it seemed familiar. It reminded her of the packets of mothballs her mother sold in the shop in Del. The little white balls were used to repel clothes moths from garments that were kept in storage.

She looked curiously after Poupette, and saw her offering the crystal bowl to Mishatweet's mother and father, who were helping themselves to nuts while Olla-Scollbow topped up their goblets from the wine jug.

So this was where the nuts "belonged"—in the stomachs of the honored guests! Another young girl, so like Poupette that the two had to be twins, was holding a plate of seafood pastries in front of Mishatweet. As Collin's bride-to-be took one pastry after another, the young girl stared at her with glazed eyes and unconsciously licked her lips.

A suspicion drifted into Britta's mind and clung there. She glanced down at the smear of liquid at the bottom of her goblet and was suddenly sure that Olla-Scollbow had known exactly what he was doing when he gave her such a tiny amount of wine. Like the nuts, the wine was not to be wasted on a stray young trader when there were more important people to be served.

"Collin's sisters are waiting on us tonight, since this is just a simple family party," Lady Poltice said loudly. "As I have already explained to our dear friends from the Isle of Jade, we have given the servants a holiday in honor of their young master's wedding."

Britta kept her smile in place, hoping it had not begun to look too false. The suspicion that had come to her was rapidly hardening into certainty. She felt a little sick as she thought of Lady Poltice's hand gripping her wrist—of the hard, rough skin she had felt hidden beneath the woman's delicate lace gloves. No fine lady with servants at her command had hands like that. Britta knew that very well—her mother was always complaining that washing clothes and scrubbing floors had ruined her hands.

So the servants were a myth. The mothball smell seemed to hint that the fine garments worn by the people of the tower were kept packed away until they were needed to impress outsiders. And plainly food and wine were not nearly as plentiful as the Olla-Scollbows wished their guests to believe.

It was almost as if the Collectors were poor—as poor as Britta's own family in Del. Certainly, despite their finery, they all looked half starved. Yet riches were all about them—the solid silver goblet in Britta's hand was proof of that.

Puzzling over the problem, Britta suddenly recalled something she had read in *A Trader's Guide to Illica*.

There was a time when the Collectors gladly paid in gold for precious objects. This is not so today. Foreign traders who ask for gold in return for any item will be treated with contempt, and informed that the Collectors of Illica trade in goods only.

Britta frowned as a startling idea struck her. What if the Collectors no longer traded in gold because they no longer *had* any gold? What if after centuries of hoarding precious objects they had no money to pay for their daily needs? What if their only fine clothes were garments handed down by their ancestors, and the only food they had was the tribute delivered by the townspeople to the tower door by night?

For the sake of pride, this strange poverty would be kept strictly secret. No important visitor to a tower would notice it, because important visitors would be always given the best of everything, while the family held back. Only an extra guest like Britta, invited only because Olla-Scollbow had not been able to resist boasting to his rival Collectors, would have a chance of guessing the truth.

Well, Britta *had* guessed it, but if she wanted to keep on Olla-Scollbow's good side she would have to pretend with all her might that she had not.

As if I do not have enough secrets to keep already, Britta thought irritably, as out of the corner of her eye she caught a glimpse of Collin gazing at her like a woebegone puppy from the other side of the room. Groaning inwardly, she turned back to Lady Poltice and again forced herself to smile.

☆

The dinner that followed the drinks was a very grand and very strained affair. The grandeur came from the huge dining room, the many courses and the masses of gleaming silver and crystal on the long table. The strain came from two different directions.

At one end of the table, anxiety radiated from Mishatweet's parents, who were clearly not sure which knife and fork they were supposed to use for each course. At the other end, the members of Olla-Scollbow's family were all pretending they were not hungry, so that most of the small supply of food could be heaped onto their guests' plates.

Britta was starving, but she managed to snare very little to eat. The twins whisked by her chair so quickly that she would have had to trip one of them up and catch the falling dish to get very much at all.

In his place of honor at the head of the table, Collin sat like a man in a trance, not even pretending to pick at the tiny portion of food on his plate. Glancing at his bent head, Britta felt a sudden, unexpected surge of sympathy.

Crossly she beat it back. Collin was marrying Mishatweet for her money, and he was abandoning the girl he really loved to do it. Such a man did not deserve pity.

She was relieved when the dinner finally ended, though she rose from the table feeling as hungry as she had when she sat down. She thought enviously of Jewel, who as a possible Bell-Slink bride had no doubt enjoyed a hearty meal in Slink Tower while the family gnawed on gristle and crusts of bread disguised in gravy.

All that remained was to plead tiredness and ask to be shown to her room. That was easily done, for Lady Poltice was plainly glad to be rid of at least one guest who might ask for more to eat and drink later on.

The twins, who had been told to guide Britta to her chamber, waited listlessly as she said goodnight to the other dinner guests.

Smothering a yawn behind her dimpled hand, Mishatweet murmured a vague response that Britta could not hear. Mishatweet's mother and father, well fed and glistening, were warm in their hopes that Britta would sleep well. Olla-Scollbow declared that he would show Britta the Collection straight after breakfast. And Collin, his eyes dark pools of misery, shook Britta's hand, secretly pressing into it a folded scrap of paper.

13 - Collin

Britta was appalled, but what could she do? She could hardly drop the note or force Collin to take it back—that would only attract unwelcome attention to both of them. Writhing with irritated fury, she had no choice but to follow the twins up the curving stone stairway, the note prickling like a spider in her sweating fist.

Alone at last in her cavernous room, with the heavy door shut, she sat on the edge of the huge, lumpy bed and made herself unfold the note. She did not want to read the thing—she wanted nothing more to do with Collin and his troubles—but of course there was no help for it. She held the note close to the flickering candle stub that the twins had left with her, and as she scanned the painfully small, cramped printing her heart sank to her boots.

I MUST SPEAK WITH YOU. I WILL COME TO YOUR CHAMBER AT MIDNIGHT. BURN THIS.

Grinding her teeth in annoyance, Britta burned the little note on the wide saucer of the candleholder. As the paper curled and grayed, and the brief flame died, the single word "midnight" seemed to leap out at her. She sighed as she pressed the fragment into ash. The evening had seemed so long that she felt it must be past midnight already, but plainly it was not. Tired to her bones, she longed to throw off her clothes and get into bed, but if Collin was to come knocking at her door that was impossible.

No doubt the wretched young man wanted to swear her to silence. If only she had not let him see that she had recognized him! Britta groaned, eased her boots from her aching feet, and lay back against the bed's one thin pillow, to wait.

The weak flame of the candle did little to light the huge room, and no moonlight filtered in through the high, narrow slit that served as a window. The hulking shapes of heavy old chests and wardrobes loomed from the bare stone walls. The stale air smelled faintly of mothballs.

Britta had meant to stay awake, but of course

she fell asleep almost at once. She was dreaming of the words engraved on the cavern wall when a scratching sound woke her with a start.

It was pitch-dark, for the candle had burned away, and for an instant she did not know where she was. Then the musty smell of the pillow reminded her. She jumped up and blundered to the door.

Collin was waiting outside, pale as the candle he held in his hand. He slid into the room like a lizard and bolted the door after him.

"In case anyone comes," he whispered. "It would not do for anyone to see me here."

"No it would not!" Britta snapped. "What do you want, Collin? Surely you have realized by now that I am not going to give you away."

"I know you must think badly of me," Collin whispered. "I had to explain—"

Britta frowned at him. "You do not owe me any explanations. Mishatweet is the one who deserves—"

"You do not understand!" Collin broke in, and his anguish was so plainly real that Britta fell silent.

"I have always loved Vorn the Ship," Collin said in a low voice. "Always—since we were children, and one day met by chance at the Blind Tower, where we had both gone to be alone. We have been meeting there in secret ever since, though we knew it was wrong. Those precious hours have been the only comfort of my life."

"Then why in the nine seas are you not marrying

Vorn, if she will have you?" Britta demanded.

Collin stared at her. "Vorn is of the town, and I am of the towers," he said, as if explaining a simple truth to a small child. "We have always known we could never marry. This afternoon we met for the last time—to say good-bye. That was what I wanted to tell you. After today, I will never see Vorn again."

His lips trembled, and Britta felt a rush of irritated pity.

"In a few short hours I will marry Mishatweet," Collin went on dully. "She is a nice enough girl. Her parents are rich and she will have a fine dowry."

"But you do not love her!" Britta exclaimed.

Collin shrugged. "She does not love me either. But she must marry someone, and her parents think it will be a fine thing to be related to a Collector of Illica." He shuddered. "If only they knew ..."

"Knew that despite all your show you have barely enough to live on, and that you only want their daughter for her money!" Britta finished for him, her contempt overwhelming both her sympathy and her caution. "You and your family are deceiving them, and in the end they will find that out."

"Yes," Collin agreed listlessly, looking down at his hands. "But by then Mishatweet and I will be wed and it will be too late. When her dowry has been spent, they will send more gold to help her and when they die she will inherit all they have left. That is how it was with my mother, in her time. That is how it has always been."

Britta could hardly believe how calmly he said it. He sounded sad, but showed not a trace of shame.

"For pity's sake, Collin, where is your honor?" she burst out. "If Scollbow Tower is so in need, why does your father not sell some of the Collection? The silver on the table tonight alone would bring in enough money to keep your family in luxury for years!"

Collin's head jerked up. He gaped at her. "*Sell?*" he repeated. "But ... we cannot *sell!* We can only trade certain items for objects that will make the Collection finer than before. The Collection must always grow. It must never become *less*."

Seeing that he was truly baffled by her suggestion, it dawned on Britta that he had been right to accuse her of not understanding. To her, his problem had seemed very simple. Now she could see that it was not.

Collin had been brought up to think that the Collection of Scollbow Tower was the most important thing in the world. Like his father before him, he had been bred to serve it. He honestly believed that it must be maintained at all costs.

"I am sorry, Collin," she said hastily. "I have no right to question your ways. The Collection is your birthright—and of course you love it and want to care for it."

"*Love* it?" The young man gave a yelp of bitter laughter. "I *hate* it! I have spent my life cleaning it, and starving for its sake. I feel sick at the thought that in time I must pass it on to my eldest child, who will be chained to it as I have been. It has robbed me of my youth, and now it has robbed me of Vorn. Oh, I wish I were dead!"

He covered his face and burst into a passion of tears.

Torn between horror at his misery and the shameful fear that someone would hear him, Britta touched his shoulder. He stiffened, and stifled his sobs.

"If you would truly rather be dead than go on living the way you do, Collin, you have nothing to lose by trying to change things, have you?" Britta said, carefully keeping any trace of pity from her voice. "There is more to life than Illica, you know. The world is wide, and full of wonders."

Collin took his hands from his tear-stained face and gazed at her for so long, and with such a strange expression, that she began to feel uneasy.

"What is it?" she was compelled to ask at last.

"Someone else said that to me once," Collin said slowly. "A man—a stranger I met at the Blind Tower—the only other person I have ever seen there except for Vorn … and you. I had almost forgotten about him, but when I saw you there today I remembered. I have been thinking of him, and of what he said, ever since."

He rubbed his eyes with his knuckles. "It was my eleventh birthday. Vorn had not been able to come to meet me and I was sad. 'Cheer up, young Collector,' the stranger said. 'You will not be a child forever, and one day you may find that there is more to life than the towers of Illica. The world is wide, and full of wonders.'"

Britta's mouth went dry.

"The stranger was tall and dark, and had eyes that sparkled, like yours," Collin went on, still staring at Britta intently. "He was in high good humor, and he smiled as if he was hugging a wonderful secret to himself. Do you know what I mean?"

Britta nodded. She could not speak. She knew without question that Collin's "stranger" had been her father. The description fitted, but far more important than that was the advice the stranger had given. Dare Larsett had said the same thing to Britta often enough, when she had raged to him over her mother's strict rules for young ladies.

"Cheer up, little bird," he would say. "One day you will be old enough to leave the nest and fly. Then you will find that there is more to life than Del harbor. The world is wide, Britta, and full of wonders."

Britta had loved to hear those words. That was why they had come so readily to her tongue. The thought gave her pain and she thrust it from her mind. She raised her eyebrows at Collin, hoping that her face showed nothing but mild interest in his tale.

"At first I was afraid," Collin went on. "I thought I had met the ghost of Blind Tower. The stranger's hands were muddy as if he had just climbed out of his grave. His fine boots were damp and covered with sand. And he had appeared out of nowhere—I had not seen him climb the hill, though I was watching, hoping to see Vorn."

He paused, gazing at Britta expectantly, waiting for her to comment.

She forced a smile, her mind racing. The picture Collin had painted told her far more than he knew. Larsett had seemed to appear "out of nowhere" and his hands were muddy—as they would have been if he had just clawed his way out of the underground stairway into the ruins. Sand was clinging to his wet boots, as it would have done if he had tramped through the sand of Bar-Enoch's death chamber. He had been smiling as if he had a wonderful secret ...

There seemed no doubt about it. When Collin saw him, Dare Larsett had just discovered the fabled Staff of Tier.

"Of course, I soon realized that the stranger was no ghost," Collin went on. "He was a man of flesh and blood, a trader who had come from the big ship moored in the bay. The ship was called the *Pride of Rosalyn*—Vorn told me that the next day."

The *Pride of Rosalyn?* Britta thought dazedly.

"How long ago was this, Collin?" she asked sharply.

Collin blinked. "It was a little over ten years ago. I know, because I was just eleven when I met the stranger, and now I am twenty-one."

He picked up his candle and went to the door. "Yes," he said, his eyes on the candle flame. "I am twenty-one. I am a grown man now. Old enough to marry. Old enough to take charge of my own life. Thank you for reminding me."

Then he was gone.

Left alone in darkness once more, Britta fell onto the lumpy bed, trying to make sense of what she had just heard. If what Collin had said was true, her father had discovered the resting place of the Staff of Tier not eight years ago, but two years before that! When he was still sailing with the Rosalyn Fleet, with Mab and Captain Mikah on the *Pride of Rosalyn*.

Slowly Britta realized how it must have been. On an ordinary trading visit to Illica, ten years ago, her father had followed the clues in the *Mysteries* book, as Sky had done. He had edged around the rocks to the turtle cave. He had found the underground stairway and Bar-Enoch's death chamber. He had seen the Staff, clutched in the pirate's wizened hands.

Then he had read the warning on the wall and seen the bones of those who had ignored it. So he had left the Staff where it lay.

But he had not intended to leave it forever.

Two years later, in secret, he had come back for it. When he was prepared. When he was his own master. When the *Star of Deltora* had been built. When a metal box lined with lead had been stored in the ship's hold …

And when he had worked out how to take the Staff from the pirate's dead hands—and survive.

14 - The Collection

Even thoughts of her father could not keep Britta awake for long, but her sleep was not peaceful. Large as it was, the chamber seemed airless, and she woke over and over again feeling she could not breathe. It was a relief when the dim light of dawn began to filter through the slit in the wall.

Yawning, she pulled on her boots, straightened her clothes and combed her tangled hair. She was wondering hungrily how soon she could venture downstairs for breakfast when she heard a timid knock. Fearing that Collin had returned, she opened the door cautiously, but her visitor was one of the twins carrying a huge silver tray.

Marooned in the center of the tray were a delicate cup of weak tea and a matching plate bearing a slice of bread and butter so thin that it was almost transparent.

"Mama thought you would prefer a light

breakfast, after the feast last night," the girl mumbled, looking everywhere but at Britta.

"You are very kind," Britta said easily, though her stomach growled at the sight of the paltry meal. As she took the tray, she wondered if the twins had had any breakfast at all. Very likely they had not, but would have to wait for any scraps left after Mishatweet and her parents had eaten their fill.

"Papa says to tell you he will come for you soon to show you the Collection," said the girl. She lifted her pinched little face and gazed up, as if she could see through the wood and stone above her head to the floors of precious objects that ruled her family's life.

Britta's stomach fluttered. Collin's strange tale of meeting her father had almost driven the importance of this morning from her mind. Now it came back to her in a rush. Today she must trade the sunrise pearl—trade it for something splendid that would win the Rosalyn contest and give her the future she had dreamed of all her life.

As she sipped the lukewarm tea and took tiny bites of the bread to make it last as long as possible, she firmly quelled her rising excitement. She had to be cool and calm when Olla-Scollbow came. Who knew what tricks he might have up his sleeve?

☆

Two hours later, Britta was feeling far from calm. Olla-Scollbow was not behaving as she had expected.

Having gallantly escorted her up to the Collection floors, he was not trying to hurry her. Nor had he pressed her to tell him what she had to trade. In fact, as he led his guest through chamber after chamber of rare, precious objects, drawing curtains back from large windows with a flourish to admit the bright morning light, he made no mention of business. He described, he praised, he gloated, but that was all.

Golden statues, gem-studded swords, weird glass shapes, antique clocks, stuffed birds and animals, exquisite furniture, ancient books, embroidered rugs, magnificent silver, fabulous jewelry, music boxes, intricate clockwork toys, curios from every island in the Silver Sea and beyond … the Collection seemed endless, and every item was different.

Britta had begun the tour taking careful note of everything and wondering how much of what she saw had been pilfered from Bar-Enoch's treasure cave. By the second floor her feet were dragging. By the third floor she was bleary-eyed and finding it hard to concentrate.

"Well, my dear, perhaps you have seen enough now, and we should get down to business," Olla-Scollbow said smoothly at last. He threw open a door right beside him. Glancing at him as he ushered her into the room beyond the door, Britta thought she caught a gleam of sly satisfaction in his eyes. Instantly she became alert.

"Here," the Collector said blandly, gesturing at

the loaded shelves, "are the items I am willing to trade. They are all rare and valuable, naturally, but they are a little like other items in the Collection, so can be spared. Sadly, some of my ancestors were careless, and collected too many things of one kind. Do you follow me?"

I follow you only too well, you old scoundrel, Britta thought grimly. You have dazzled, exhausted and confused me, showing me thousands of things I cannot have. Now you hope that you have softened me up enough for me to make a bad decision.

But she merely smiled and looked vaguely around, trying to appear as tired and off-guard as her host intended her to be.

"So many beautiful things ..." she murmured.

And most of the objects truly *were* beautiful—exquisitely beautiful. Those that were not beautiful were strange and fascinating. Some, as Olla-Scollbow had said, looked rather like items Britta remembered seeing in other rooms. Others she did not recognize—but of course she had not seen the whole Collection. Mercifully, she had been spared that.

She hitched her shore bag more firmly over her shoulder and saw her host's eyes narrow. Good. He thought her trade item was in the bag. He would be all the more astonished when she dipped into her pocket and casually pulled out one of the most precious things to be found in the Silver Sea.

She walked slowly along the shelves, looking carefully at everything. Olla-Scollbow was chattering beside her, but she did not really listen. She was staring, judging, letting her instincts guide her.

She stopped before a small, perfect model of a tree. The gnarled trunk and spreading branches of the tree were gold. Its leaves were of jade, every leaf finely carved, and between the leaves shone bell-shaped fruit made of golden topaz.

Glancing at Olla-Scollbow for permission, Britta picked up the little tree. At the touch of her fingers, the topaz fruit glowed, and a soft, sighing song filled the air.

Britta gazed at the beautiful, singing thing in her hand and knew it was what she had been looking for. It was very heavy for its size, and it did not look to her as if the gold was merely a coating over some other metal. Besides, the object itself was so perfect in every detail, and radiated such magic, that she knew it would be very highly valued in Del even if the trunk were not solid gold.

"You have good taste, my dear," Olla-Scollbow said, sounding a little startled. "But I fear your taste may be beyond your means. The artist, from the Isle of Dorne, made only two bell-fruit trees, and the other is only slightly more valuable than this, because it is a little larger."

Britta smiled slightly, and put the tree down. Moving on to glance with pretended interest at a jeweled water jug with a stopper shaped like a flying fish, she slipped her hand into her pocket and took the sunrise pearl between her fingertips. Now was her moment.

And then, just as she was about to turn back to Olla-Scollbow and spring her surprise, she saw the shallow velvet-covered box that lay open on the shelf beside the water jug. Her fingers froze.

The box held a collection of large, perfect pearls—pearls that blushed with the pink of sunrise.

"Oh, yes," said Olla-Scollbow carelessly, following the direction of her eyes. "Those are sunrise pearls—from the island of Two Moons, you know. My great-great-grandmother was mad for them. They are extremely valuable, of course—far more so than when they came into the Collection—but we have too many for our needs. Now, I do not want to hurry you, but I really must be getting on, to dress for the wedding. Have you seen anything else you like?"

Britta was so devastated that she could not speak. Olla-Scollbow frowned and began to tap his foot.

"I—I will have to think about it," she managed to say after a moment.

"As you wish," the man said, with a tight little smile. "But if you imagine you will find better in another Tower, I must warn you that the Scollbow Collection is judged by all the traders who matter to be the best and most varied in Illica."

"I—I am sure," Britta babbled, thinking of nothing but getting away.

As she turned to go, the door of the room flew

open. Lady Poltice was standing there, her face a mask of fury.

"Look at this!" she almost screamed, waving a sheet of paper at her husband. "How could he do it? How *could* he?"

Elbowing roughly past Britta, Olla-Scollbow snatched the paper from his wife's hand. In a shaking voice, he read aloud:

Dear Mama and Papa,

I am sorry to disappoint you, but I cannot marry the bride you have chosen for me. I love Vorn the Ship, and have gone with her to seek my fortune. The stranger's words have made me see that this is right. There is more to life than the towers of Illica.

I hope you will find it in your hearts to forgive me and wish me well. Please give my apologies to Mishatweet and her parents, though I am sure that when they learn more about our family, they will realize that they have had a lucky escape.

Collin

"You!" shrieked Lady Poltice, jabbing a shaking, bony finger at Britta. "You did this! You turned our son against us! 'The stranger,' he says. 'The stranger' told him to run off with a vulgar town girl, instead of doing his duty! And you, a guest in our house! You—you viper!"

In that instant, Britta knew there was nothing to be done. She was not "the stranger" Collin had meant in his note, but she would never be able to convince anyone of that. It hardly mattered anyway, for she had offered Collin the same advice as her father had done.

So she obeyed her instincts, and fled. She ducked around Olla-Scollbow, who was spluttering with baffled rage. She dodged Lady Poltice, who lashed out at her as she passed. She found the staircase and ran down to the ground floor, taking the steps two at a time.

At the bottom of the stairs she almost collided with the twins, who were clinging together, one in tears and the other laughing. As she hurried past the dining room she caught a glimpse of Mishatweet's parents talking together in scandalized voices, and Mishatweet herself, placidly eating sugared dates.

Then the entrance hall was before her. In moments, with relief that could not be described, she was bursting out of the tower door into the glorious open air.

Her head spinning, her hair flying behind her, she ran down the hill to the jetty. There was the *Star of Deltora,* waiting to receive her. Never had she seen such a welcome sight. Less welcome was the sight of Mab, who was standing on deck with Healer Kay and Captain Hara, gazing somberly at a scene of uproar in the nearby boatyard.

As Britta stumbled, panting, up the gangplank, Mab and the others turned to look at her.

"This is a very sudden arrival, Britta," Mab said, a touch of frost in her voice. "Have you completed your trade?"

"N-no," stammered Britta, pressing her fingers to the stitch in her side. "Master Olla-Scollbow had no need of—of what I had to offer." She winced, reliving the sick shock she had felt on seeing the little heap of pink pearls in the velvet box. What would she do if the other Collectors also had more sunrise pearls than they wanted?

"I see." Mab's eyes narrowed. "And is that all you have to tell me of your time in Scollbow Tower?"

Wilting before the old trader's hard stare, Britta opened her mouth and shut it again. She glanced at Kay's troubled face and found no comfort there.

"Very early this morning," Mab said evenly, "we heard of a scandal that has now set tongues wagging all over the town. It seems that Vorn the Ship eloped with Olla-Scollbow's son last night. The girl left a note saying that she had taken some supplies and a boat as payment for her work in the family's business over many years. And, sure enough, a sailing boat is missing—Vorn's favorite of the many she built herself."

"A neat craft, so Brett the Ship tells me, but very small and light—fit only for fishing in the harbor," Hara rumbled. "The young fools will not last a week in the open sea. I had always thought Vorn was a person of sense, but it seems I was wrong."

Cold with horror, Britta turned to look at the boatyard, where figures in blue were dashing about, or gathered together arguing and stabbing their fingers at maps spread out between them.

"The Ship clan is in turmoil, of course," Mab said. "I imagine that the people of Scollbow Tower are in an even worse state. Unless they do not yet know what has happened." She raised her eyebrows at Britta.

Britta wet her lips. "They found out not long ago," she said stiffly. "Collin left a note also. And I—I am afraid they blame me for what happened."

"I knew it!" Mab muttered, exchanging glances with Kay. "Britta, you little blockhead! Did I not tell you—?"

"But, truly, Mab, it was not all my fault!" Britta broke in desperately. "Collin did not want to marry the bride his parents had found for him. He and Vorn—"

"Save your breath!" Mab snapped. "By the look of things, you will need to explain yourself soon enough, and I have no wish to hear about this folly twice."

She jerked her head in the direction of Scollbow Tower. Britta looked up, and her stomach turned over as she saw the thin, dark figures of Olla-Scollbow and

Lady Poltice almost running down the hill.

They were gesturing violently as they came, and soon it was clear that they were calling out too. Their cries drifted down to the ship, harsh as the screeches of fighting birds, but at first Britta could not make out any actual words. Then, as the running pair reached the bottom of the hill, she heard Captain Hara curse under his breath, and the next moment she too realized what was being shouted to the winds.

"Raise the Jaws!" Olla-Scollbow and his wife were shrieking. "Raise—the—Jaws!"

15 - No Refuge

Mab caught the word "Jaws" an instant later. She gave a low groan and shut her eyes, swaying a little where she stood. Beneath the paint, her seamed face was bleached. Hara and Healer Kay both grunted in alarm and moved quickly to support her.

Britta felt a stab of fear. Never before had she seen Mab give way like this. It was as shocking to her as if the *Star of Deltora*'s deck had suddenly begun to quake and crumble beneath her feet. She realized with a kind of wonder how much she had come to depend on the old trader's strength.

"Get Mab below, Kay!" Hara barked. "Take the girl with you."

"No!" Mab's eyes opened. With an effort she straightened her back, pushing herself away from Healer Kay. "We must face this and have done with it. If it drags on it will cause delay we cannot afford. Britta, stay by me! And keep silent unless I tell you otherwise."

She glanced at the boatyard. The people there had seen the approaching Collectors, and were pointing and muttering angrily.

"With luck, Brett the Ship will not be in the mood to listen to demands from Scollbow Tower this morning," Kay murmured.

"With luck." Hara looked doubtful. "But when a Collector demands that the Jaws be raised—"

"The Collector must have good reason," Mab said sharply. "Illica's savage days are over. Ships cannot be trapped inside the bay on a Collector's spiteful whim any longer, and this demand is pure spite, if ever I saw it! Whatever Britta might have said to that fool of a bridegroom, it could not have made him act against his will."

She was speaking as if Britta was not there. Her whole attention was on Olla-Scollbow and Lady Poltice, who were now pounding onto the jetty. They were both panting heavily, no longer able to speak, let alone to shout.

The people in the boatyard were shouting, though—shouting and shaking their fists. Then, as if someone had given a signal, they began swarming onto the jetty.

Other townspeople, attracted by the noise, came running from the street. Hearing mutters behind her,

Britta glanced round and saw that the members of the crew who had stayed on board had moved closer to the gangplank and were watching curiously. Sky was with them and, to Britta's surprise, so was Jewel, towering over the rest. So Jewel, too, had returned early to the ship.

There was no time to wonder why. No time to do more than give Jewel a rueful shrug before turning back to face the jetty. Lady Poltice and her husband had reached the bottom of the gangplank. They paid no attention to the crowd gathering behind them. They were still unable to speak, but their furious eyes as they glared up at Britta spoke for them.

"Stay where you are," Mab muttered to Kay. Keeping Britta close beside her, she moved to the head of the gangplank and nodded to the Collectors.

"Greetings, Lady Poltice, Master Olla-Scollbow," she said calmly. "Can I be of assistance?"

"That—that girl ..." gasped Olla-Scollbow, pointing at Britta

"What do you mean by showing your face down here, Collector?" bawled a burly man in blue, shouldering his way to the front of the crowd. "Your cursed son's stolen my daughter away! Sailed off through the channel, they have—in one of our best boats too!"

The crowd muttered angrily and pressed forward. Olla-Scollbow, still barely able to speak, bared his teeth.

"We'll never find them now!" the man in blue bellowed. "They're both as good as dead. And Vorn the handiest little worker in the yard!"

The muttering in the crowd rose to a rolling growl.

Britta looked down at the sea of furious faces. The townspeople were shocked and outraged. Perhaps later they would be grief stricken at the thought of Vorn and Collin at sea in a tiny boat. But for now all they could think of was that a girl from the town had fallen in love with the son of a Collector, and the very idea filled them with disgust.

Traditions are all-important in Illica.

Mab had said that, and *A Trader's Guide to Illica* had said much the same thing. But now, for the first time, Britta realized that she had not taken the phrase seriously enough.

Traditions in Illica were not like the traditions of Del—respected, but able to be broken in cases of real need. They were not even like ordinary laws. They were set so hard in people's minds that they had come to seem more like laws of nature. The tide rose and fell. Crops needed rain. Certain seabirds nested on the cliffs at certain times of the year. Collectors did not marry people of the town.

And suddenly Britta saw with shame how wrong she had been to think of Collin as weak. Collin had been struggling against forces more powerful than she had dreamed of—his own conscience not the least. And Vorn … Vorn had looked practical and determined, but she no doubt had had her own bitter battle with the teaching of a lifetime before agreeing to run away with him.

Vorn's father was still roaring from the jetty, heaping insults on Olla-Scollbow's head, cursing the day Collin was born.

"This sly foreign girl—this witch—is to blame!" Lady Poltice shrieked, jabbing her finger at Britta. "She cast a spell on our son, making him abandon his beloved bride on the eve of their wedding! And now we know why! She used our horror and distraction on finding his note to steal from us! She *stole* from the Collection!"

And abruptly, there was utter silence on the jetty. Vorn's father froze, his mouth gaping, his fist still raised.

Mab stiffened. As Hara moved quickly to her side, she turned to Britta, her hooded eyes startled.

"I do not know what she is talking about!" Britta cried indignantly. "I did not steal anything!"

"Of course she did not. There must be some mistake," she heard Healer Kay exclaim, and felt a dizzying wave of gratitude.

"Mistake or not, this is trouble, Mab," Hara muttered. "To steal from a Collection is the worst of crimes on Illica. Worse than murder."

"I know that as well as you do, Hara!" Mab hissed. "By all the little fishes, what next? Britta, are you *certain* that you did not accidentally—"

"I touched nothing!" Britta insisted. "Well, except for a little gold tree, and Olla-Scollbow saw me put that back."

With a pang she thought of the haunting song of the tree, and the bell-shaped topaz fruit that had glowed beneath her fingers.

"This ship cannot leave the bay until our property is returned to us!" screamed Lady Poltice. "Raise the Jaws! The Collectors of Scollbow Tower demand it!"

"Mab!" Hara growled urgently.

Mab turned back to face the crowd. "I fear there has been some confusion," she said, expertly pitching her voice so that every word could be heard on the jetty. "Lady Poltice, Master Olla-Scollbow, please come aboard so we can get to the truth of this matter."

Watched in silence by the crowd, the Collectors stamped up the gangplank.

"Now," said Mab, still in that calm but carrying voice, "what exactly are you accusing Britta of stealing?"

Olla-Scollbow found his voice at last. "A sunrise pearl!" he wheezed. "While I was comforting my wife, the girl stole a sunrise pearl and ran from the tower."

"That is not true!" cried Britta, heat rushing into her face as behind her the crew exclaimed in shock.

"It is!" Olla-Scollbow spluttered. "Do you deny that you were looking with great interest at the sunrise pearls available for trade when my wife came in? Do you deny that at the time you were standing right beside the box in which they were kept?"

Britta felt a small, cold stab of fear, but she kept her face expressionless. "No, I do not deny it," she replied evenly. "But—"

"Hah!" roared Olla-Scollbow. "Then can you explain the fact that there were eight pearls in that box, but when we counted them after you had gone, there were only seven?"

The people on the jetty shouted aloud, but this time their shocked anger was not directed at Olla-Scollbow. Now, despite their horror at Vorn and Collin's escape, they were as one with the Collectors of Scollbow Tower. Their fury was for Britta, the foreigner accused of breaking their most ancient law.

"Well?" Lady Poltice shrieked, poking her head at Britta like a starved bird of prey. "Can you explain it?"

And suddenly Britta had had enough. Suddenly the tangled emotions of the day before, the confusion of the night, the crushing disappointment of the morning and the anger at being accused of theft came together in a red wave of fury.

"Of course I can explain it!" she flashed back. "And so could you if you thought about it for a single moment! If a sunrise pearl is missing, plainly Collin took it!"

A great cry rose from the jetty. Lady Poltice screamed and recoiled as if Britta were a venomous snake. Olla-Scollbow became very still.

"Do—you dare to suggest that the son of a Collector family would *steal* from the Collection?" he rasped.

By now Britta knew that she would have done better to hold her tongue, but she was unable to see a way of taking back what she had said. All she could do was go on.

"When did you last count the pearls in that box, Master Olla-Scollbow?" she spat. "How do you know there were eight there this morning? How do you know that Collin did not take one in the night, before he fled? He might well have seen a sunrise pearl as fair exchange for years of slavery to that wretched Collection."

The people on the jetty howled and hissed, shaking their fists at Britta and pressing closer and closer to the ship. Olla-Scollbow's mouth was opening and closing like the mouth of a gasping fish. He looked really ill, and his wife looked no better.

"Be calm, I beg you," Mab shouted over the uproar. "I apologize for the girl—she is young—she does not know what she is saying. Naturally the son of a Tower would never plunder a Collection. But there are many ways in which a small item like a pearl could have been mislaid. It might have simply fallen from the box during cleaning and rolled into a corner unnoticed."

"Impossible!" cried Olla-Scollbow. "It is our children's duty to clean the Collection, and they are trained from the time they can walk to—"

"It is my duty to clear the name of someone from this ship who has been accused of a very serious crime!" Mab cut in. "And there is a very simple way to do that. Britta came aboard only shortly before you did, Master Olla-Scollbow. Captain Hara and Healer Kay can join me in testifying that she has not moved from this spot since her arrival."

She turned to Britta. "Please hand your shore bag to Lady Poltice, so she can search it," she said curtly.

And only then did Britta realize the full extent of her danger. She stood motionless, shocked that in her anger she had failed to see how her ordeal might end. This cannot be happening, she thought. It cannot …

"Britta!" Mab barked.

Numbly, Britta handed over the bag. She felt only faintly humiliated as Lady Poltice, her nose pinched with distaste, pulled out the old blue skirt, the water flask and a handful of hairpins. It was as if the paltry contents of the bag belonged to someone else.

"There!" said Mab, as Lady Poltice let the bag fall to the deck and brushed her hands as if they had been contaminated. "I hope you are satisfied."

But Britta remembered Lady Poltice's gimlet eyes noting every detail of her appearance when they met, and waited for the blow she knew must fall.

"I am far from satisfied!" Lady Poltice cried shrilly. "The girl's skirt has secret pockets—one on each side, above the flounce. I demand she turn out her pockets!"

And there it was. How strange, Britta thought, that now the moment she had been dreading had come, she felt very little.

She did not wait for Mab's order. She bent and unbuttoned the right-hand pocket of her skirt. There was no point in delaying the moment of truth. Both pockets would be searched at last, that was certain, and why show the goozli, hidden in the left-hand pocket, when there was no need?

Watched closely by Lady Poltice, Britta turned the pocket inside out. Slowly the contents were revealed: a comb, a notebook and pencil … and, carefully wrapped in a handkerchief, a large, perfect pink pearl.

16 - Two Evils

Lady Poltice screamed in triumph. Olla-Scollbow bared his teeth. The people on the jetty howled. Britta looked at Mab—at Mab's haggard face, which had become as rigid as a mask carved out of wood, every line and furrow deeply etched. She roused herself.

"This pearl is mine," she said, speaking directly to the old trader and ignoring everyone else. "I brought it here from Two Moons. I had hoped to trade it this morning, but then I found that the Scollbow Collection had too many sunrise pearls already."

"Oh, really!" Olla-Scollbow sneered. "You bought a sunrise pearl in Two Moons, did you? Well, you can prove that easily enough. Show us your receipt!"

"I have no receipt," said Britta, her eyes still fixed on Mab. "I did not buy the pearl. I found it in the Two Moons swamplands."

She heard a chorus of gasps and curses from the crew gathered behind her. Muttered words and phrases floated to her ears. "She … the turtle people … the mark of Tier …"

Britta did not look round. She knew that Olla-Scollbow and his wife were jeering, but she did not look at them either. She kept her eyes on Mab's face, willing Mab to believe her.

Mab's lips opened. "Nonsense!" she snapped. "Never have I heard such a tale! Master Olla-Scollbow, Lady Poltice, it seems I must apologize. I have been deceived. If your property is returned to you, may I presume that you will leave the punishment of this girl to me?"

The Collectors glanced at each other then nodded with bad grace.

"Britta, hand back the pearl," Mab said.

Britta's heart gave a great, painful thud. She closed her fingers over the precious thing that was her future, and held it tightly. "No!" she gasped. "It is mine! I found it! It is mine! Mab, I beg you—"

"Hand the pearl back to its rightful owners this minute or it will be taken from you by force." Mab's voice was very cold. Her eyes, hard as polished stones, seemed to be staring straight through Britta. She turned her head slightly and said something to Captain Hara. He moved forward and stood between Britta and the scowling Collectors.

"Give it up, girl," Hara muttered, his rough voice

strangely gentle. "There's no help for it now. Don't make me hurt you." He held out his hand.

And Britta knew that the fight was over. She had lost and there was nothing to be done. She opened her fingers and tipped the pearl onto Hara's broad palm. As if she were living in a dream she watched him turn and give the pearl to Olla-Scollbow.

Dimly she heard Lady Poltice crow in triumph, heard the crowd on the jetty cheer and hiss. She heard Mab give orders that the *Star of Deltora* was to leave Illica with the smallest possible delay. She heard the ship's bell clanging, urgently summoning Vashti and the crew who were still ashore. She heard Mab tell her to get below, to go to her cabin and to stay there.

And blindly Britta went. She went steadily, her head held high. She did not notice the crew shrinking back as she passed. She did not see Jewel and Sky looking after her. She thought of nothing but putting one foot before the other, as if to stumble would be the worst thing that could happen to her.

But when at last the cabin door had closed behind her, her knees began to tremble. Holding on to the wall for support, she crept like an old woman to the writing table and lowered herself into her usual seat. Still her mind was strangely blank. Shadows were flickering around her, pressing close, but she did not find them disturbing. They were quite comforting, in fact. They are only memories, after all, she thought vaguely, remembering Sky's words in the cavern.

Still, it was odd that memories trapped in the cabin walls could bring her comfort. It came to her that the shadows seemed to be grieving for her in her trouble. They did not understand quite what that trouble was, only that she felt empty, lost and very alone. They wanted to fill the emptiness, to wrap her in their ghostly arms and press closer, closer …

The goozli twitched in Britta's pocket. She roused herself with a start. The shadows drew back as she took the little figure from her pocket and stood it on the tabletop in front of her.

The goozli bowed. When it straightened, its small black eyes looked grave.

"The pearl you found for me is gone, goozli," Britta murmured. "They took it. They said I was a thief."

The little creature lifted its shoulders in a faint shrug. It touched its forehead, and then its heart.

"Yes, I still have you," said Britta, and was surprised to feel the corners of her mouth curving into a small, rueful smile. The lost, empty feeling grew less. At the same time, she became aware of changes in the movement of the ship, and realized that the *Star* was drawing away from the jetty. Hara had wasted no time in following Mab's orders.

There was a sound outside the cabin. The goozli froze as Jewel stalked in, closed the door behind her and glared at Britta.

"I did not steal that pearl, Jewel," Britta said in a low voice.

Jewel sighed and put her hands on her hips.

"I am telling the truth!" Britta cried. "Whatever Mab thinks, I am no thief!"

"I know that!" Jewel said impatiently. "Sky knows it, Hara knows it, Kay knows it … and Mab knows it too. Of course we do—how stupid do you think we are? Plainly Olla-Scollbow's wretched son took the pearl—just as his ladylove took the boat. He took it to fund their new life, I daresay. Not that they will *have* a new life, or any life at all, by the sound of things."

She shook her head in disgust as Britta stared at her, dumbfounded.

"Do you not see, Britta? Above all things, Mab has to get the *Star of Deltora* home. If you had not given up the pearl, the Jaws would have been raised and we would have been trapped in Illica harbor for who knows how long. Those people were not in a mood to see reason."

"They might have done, at last, if Mab had stood by me!" Britta burst out, almost choking on the flood of bitter resentment that had risen in her throat. "Instead, she chose to shame and rob me. If she truly believed me when I said I had found the pearl—"

"By the stars, Britta, have you no sense at all?" Jewel exploded. "Do you not see that once you claimed you had *found* the wretched pearl, instead of making up some other tale about how you came by it, Mab had no choice but to call you a liar? She had to think quickly, and she chose the lesser of two evils. The crew was suspicious enough of you before. But when you said what you did …" She trailed off, scowling.

Britta remembered the men muttering fearfully behind her.

She … the turtle people … the Mark of Tier …

She turned and looked into the mirror above the writing table. Her hair, tossed by the breeze as she ran to the ship, fell in dark, tangled locks over the blazing silk of her blouse. Her bangs had been blown to one side and the amber mark stood out like a brand on her brow.

"You mean … the men might think I used Tier's sorcery to find the pearl—as the turtle people are said to do?" she faltered.

"Of course!" hissed Jewel. "And it is better by far—safer for you and for all of us—for them to think you are a liar and a thief."

She grimaced. "I only hope Mab's act convinced them. I did not believe it for a moment—you were so plainly speaking the truth. But then, I know you—or thought I did."

Britta met her eyes in the mirror. There was hurt in Jewel's steady brown gaze.

"I cannot believe that you did not tell me of the pearl," Jewel muttered. "You said you had learned to keep things to yourself, but how could you have kept quiet about a thing like that? You are a deep one, Britta, and no mistake! It makes me wonder what other secrets you are keeping."

"You yourself once reminded me that we were rivals in the Rosalyn contest and should be wary of what we told each other!" Britta exclaimed, stung. "I have no idea what *your* trades have been!"

Jewel smiled without humor. "I think a miracle like finding a sunrise pearl is rather different. If it had happened to me, I would not have thought twice about telling you. I could not have kept it to myself. And as for my trades—well, there was only one trade, in Two Moons, and now there will be no other. It is not the result I had planned for."

She dropped into the other seat and planted her elbows on the tabletop, resting her chin on her hands and staring broodingly at the goozli.

"It may not be the result you planned for, Jewel, but I would rather be in your shoes than mine," Britta could not help saying with a touch of bitterness. "Vashti is your only rival in the contest now. And who is to say that she bought better in Two Moons than you did?"

Jewel said nothing.

"You did not see anything you wanted in Slink Tower?" asked Britta, to break the silence.

"I did not see anything at all." Jewel hunched her shoulders. "The evening was a nightmare. The Bell-Slink woman thrust her miserable son at me at every turn, and she and her daughters fawned over me till it was all I could do not to knock their heads together. As if I could be flattered into marrying a feeble bag of bones who was plainly terrified by the very sight of me!"

"But—did you not see the Collection this morning?"

Jewel flung herself back in her chair, and sighed. "I might as well tell you—you will hear about it from Sky soon enough. The fact is, I am in disgrace too. Mab will never have me as her Apprentice now, even if my Two Moons purchase *is* more valuable than Vashti's."

Britta caught her breath, her own troubles forgotten for the moment. "Jewel! Do not tell me that you lost your temper with Madam Bell-Slink at last!"

"Not quite." Jewel rubbed her painted skull ruefully. "But I did something almost as bad. After this terrible evening, they put me in a bedchamber that was like a dungeon. There was no light and no air. I could not stay there—I thought I would suffocate. So when they were all asleep I broke out of the tower and came back to the ship."

"Broke out?" Britta repeated, stunned.

"Forced the lock on the front door and ran for my life." Jewel shook her head and despite everything gave a snort of laughter. "It was a ridiculous thing to do, but I was beyond thought by then, I think. Sky was on night watch, so I was able to board and get below without fuss. But in the morning, when I had come to my senses, I tried to get back on shore and Mab caught me at it. Then Bell-Slink arrived on the jetty breathing fire, and it was all up with me."

"Oh, Jewel!" Britta clapped her hand to her mouth.

Jewel began to laugh in earnest. "Mab had to pay for the broken lock then and there. She told me to get out of her sight and has not spoken to me since. Ah, well ..."

She wiped her eyes with the back of her hand. "I feel a fool for showing such weakness. I squirm to think how my brothers will laugh at me when they hear of it. But in truth if being the Rosalyn Apprentice means putting up with the antics of people like the Bell-Slinks, Vashti is welcome to the job!"

"Well, it seems that she is going to get it," Britta said bitterly, her hands curling into fists at the thought of Vashti's father gaining control over the *Star of Deltora*. "Sky is disqualified, you are disgraced, and even if Mab forgives me for the trouble with Collin, I have nothing to show the Trust Committee—nothing to show for my ten gold coins."

Jewel brightened. "But *I* have something, little nodnap, and it is no use to me now!" she exclaimed. "I could give it to you, and then you could—" Her face fell and she shook her head. "Oh no, that will not do—the receipt is in my name."

Britta's heart warmed, but before she could say anything there was a tap on the door and Sky sidled into the cabin.

"I have come with an urgent message for Britta the pearl thief," he drawled with a mocking smile. "Or should that be Britta the turtle witch, terror of the Silver Sea?"

17 - A Long Way Back to Del

Jewel frowned. "Do not joke, Sky!" she muttered, with a sideways glance at Britta's stricken face. "Have the men accepted Mab's story? Do they believe that Britta stole the sunrise pearl?"

Sky sobered instantly. "Some do," he said. "But Crow and his cronies are convinced that Britta found the pearl by sorcery. Hara is jeering at the idea, but so far he has done little good. Mab would do better, if she was well, but the scene on the jetty seems to have been too much for her. Kay bundled her below the moment we cast off."

"Why are you here?" Jewel asked bluntly. "Are you not wanted on deck?"

"Not until we have passed through the channel. In the meantime, Hara sent me to warn you not to leave your cabin, Britta, on any account, till things simmer down. He will have your meals sent to you here."

"It is not fair," Britta muttered. "I am not a witch, or a thief. Why should I be punished?"

"Hara has no choice," said Sky. "The situation is not good."

"It certainly is not," Jewel agreed. "How Hara and Mab must regret giving the *Star*'s regular crew leave, and taking on a new one for this voyage! The usual men know Hara well, and have learned to trust him. This crew is another matter. You should never have admitted to finding that pearl, Britta."

"But I did not find it by sorcery!" Britta burst out. "It was caught in my hair, clotted with mud, after I fell into the swamp."

"Caught in your hair?" Sky laughed. "You have a talent for finding things, and no mistake! Speaking of which, last night I cleaned the treasures you found in Bar-Enoch's chamber. They are even more valuable than I thought at first. All being well, I will be able to sell them for a very tidy sum."

As he spoke, he tweaked one of the little ornaments tied to his braids—the one shaped like a coin—and suddenly Britta realized what the ornaments were. They were lucky charms!

"So the coin charm brings good fortune in matters of money, Sky," she murmured. "You have your own superstitions, it seems."

With some satisfaction she saw Sky wince, as if he had been found out in something embarrassing. It was good to shake his superior composure for once.

And in some strange way the fact that he wore and believed in lucky charms made her feel that she knew him better.

"In the Mere, where I come from, everyone wears charms that are supposed to bring good fortune in different parts of life," Sky mumbled, recovering a little. "I cannot say that my money charm has brought me luck in the past, but lately it seems to have come into its own."

"I am glad of it," Britta said, and for Sky's sake she truly was, though even thinking about the goozli's finds in Bar-Enoch's death chamber made her shudder. Like Jewel, she would not have touched that tainted gold again for anything, whatever it was worth.

"On deck earlier I thought I knew why you would not take your proper share of that treasure," Sky went on. "You had a sunrise pearl in your pocket all the time—a pearl worth a fortune!"

Britta kept silent, feeling the color rise in her cheeks.

"But then I found that you were not going to sell the pearl on the quiet when we returned to Del, as I would have done," Sky persisted, watching her keenly. "You planned to trade it in Illica for something that would win the Rosalyn contest. And to me that means that you wanted to win the contest more than anything else in the world."

Britta nodded, swallowing the hard lump that had risen in her throat.

"What are you playing at, Sky?" hissed Jewel. "Stop tormenting her!"

Sky looked startled then shook his head impatiently. "I did not mean to torment her. I simply wanted to explain to her why she should accept this."

He passed Britta a small object folded in a piece of notepaper.

Wondering, Britta opened the paper. Into her hand fell the hair clip found with the gold in Bar-Enoch's chamber. Sky had washed it clean of sand, and seeing it for the first time in daylight, Britta caught her breath.

The clip was not set with chips of sapphire, as she had thought, but with tiny blue seashells arranged in a swirling pattern of lines that seemed to have no beginning and no end.

"Sky!" she breathed, gently touching the shells with the tip of one finger. "Can these be …?"

"Odi shells? I think so," said Sky. "I have seen pictures … And that pattern—"

"Is traditional," Jewel finished for him. "In Maris it means 'Forever.'"

She shrugged as her companions glanced at her in surprise. "My aunt has an odi shell pendant very like that clip. It was her marriage token."

Britta stared down at the shining clip, wondering why she did not feel the same revulsion for it as she did for the other things the goozli had found in the death chamber. All she felt was wonder at its beauty, and warmth at the thought of small webbed Maris hands patiently setting the delicate shells into the thin gold frame.

What had Sven said of odi shells in *A Trader's Life?*

It is said that a small number of the tiny blue shells called "odi" are washed up on the Maris shore only once every seven years, always on the night of the full moon. Odi ornaments are highly prized as love tokens because the shells are so rare and their marvelous color, blue as the eternal sky, never fades.

"It is nowhere near as precious as a sunrise pearl, of course," she heard Sky saying, "but it should impress the Rosalyn Committee."

"I should say so!" Jewel agreed with enthusiasm. "It must be far more valuable than whatever Vashti bought in Two Moons."

She swung round as Britta made a small, protesting sound. "Now do not make difficulties, Britta!" she scolded. "You found the treasure in Bar-Enoch's cave—you deserve to profit by it."

"But I—I cannot use the clip as my trade," Britta stammered. "I—I found it. I did not trade for it."

"You certainly did," Sky retorted. "You traded for it with me, and you have the receipt to prove it. See?"

He tapped the paper that had been wrapped

around the clip. Britta read the words written there.

Supplied to Britta of Del:
1 gold hair clip set with odi shells

In trade for:
2 gold coins + 1 embroidered coin purse

Sky of Rithmere

"Sky," she protested, half laughing, "we cannot—"

"You traded with the turtle people for my life," Sky broke in firmly. "So I left Two Moons owing you two gold coins and an embroidered coin purse. The treasure from Bar-Enoch's cave became mine when you gave it to me. Now I have exchanged part of that treasure for the debt. It is a perfectly fair and honorable trade, even if we did not haggle over it."

Jewel hooted with laughter. "Perfectly fair!" she exclaimed. "But will the Trust Committee accept it?"

"I do not see why not." Sky grinned. "I am no longer a finalist, so I suppose I am as good a trading partner as any. Vashti's father will protest, of course, but Sorrel may well overrule him."

"If that happens, Loy is sure to raise the scandal of Olla-Scollbow's stolen pearl," Jewel put in reluctantly. "And he will try to blame Britta for the deaths of those poor young lovers who ran away."

Sky glanced at Britta, who had turned very pale.

He hesitated briefly, then shrugged. "Mab knows the truth about the pearl and she can tell it, once we are safely home. As for the other … from what I hear, Vorn the Boat is no fool. I am willing to bet that she knows exactly what she is doing, and that in the end she and Collin will be found alive and well."

"Oh, if only that could be so!" Britta cried.

"It *will* be so, I know it," Sky said firmly. And though Britta's common sense told her that he could not know any such thing, she felt absurdly comforted.

"Now, can I tell Hara you will follow his orders and stay here for the time being?" Sky asked. He waited for Britta's sober nod then turned to go, but halfway through the doorway he impulsively looked back. "Be of good heart, Britta," he said. "It may look now as if the odds are against us, but who knows what the voyage home will bring? Anything might happen."

Britta looked at him quickly. There had been something in his voice …

"Sky, what are you planning?" Jewel asked suspiciously. "Nothing foolhardy, I hope. We are all in enough trouble as it is."

"I am not *planning* anything," Sky drawled. "I am simply reminding you that the game is not over before the last dice have been thrown. Luck can change in an instant, for good or ill. And it is a long way back to Del."

He nodded and escaped before they could ask him any more.

"What a strange, slippery fish he is!" Jewel murmured. "Who knows—" She paused, her head on one side as if she was listening, then jumped up, strode to the porthole and pulled back the curtain.

"Ah, I thought so!" she exclaimed. "We are through that cursed channel. Thank the stars, little nodnap! We are on our way home!"

Thank the stars, Britta thought, looking from the tall figure at the porthole to the little odi clip glittering in the palm of her hand. Thank the stars for true friends.

Soft shadows brushed her skin and stirred her hair. Longing whispers breathed in the air around her. *Home … home … home …*

They did not trouble Britta. She barely heard them. Her ears were filling with the sounds of the *Star of Deltora* joyfully greeting the open sea. She was imagining her ship's great sails unfurling, catching the wind. Her heart was swelling with hope and at the same time knocking with fear as Sky's last words echoed in her mind.

… the game is not over before the last dice have been thrown. Luck can change in an instant, for good or ill. And it is a long way back to Del.

DON'T MISS THE ELECTRIFYING CONCLUSION TO THE *STAR OF DELTORA* SERIES!

BOOK 4: THE HUNGRY ISLE

The *Star of Deltora* has escaped Illica, but home and safety are still very far away. The shadows that haunt the ship are deepening. Strange currents, seen and unseen, are sweeping Britta and her friends into peril.

The magic Staff of Tier has sensed them, the Hungry Isle is on the prowl, and Britta's dreams of winning the Rosalyn Apprentice contest will soon be swamped in a tidal wave of terror.

Lives hang in the balance and shock follows shock as Britta's quest to escape her past reaches its tumultuous climax.

Book 4 in the spellbinding Star of Deltora Series.

AND WHERE THE STORY BEGAN ...

BOOK 1: SHADOWS OF THE MASTER

Britta has always wanted to be trader like her father, sailing the nine seas and bringing precious cargo home to Del harbor. Her dreams seemed safe until her father's quest to find the fabled Staff of Tier ended in blood and horror. Now his shamed family is in hiding, and his ship, the *Star of Deltora,* belongs to the powerful Rosalyn fleet. But Britta's ambition burns as fiercely as ever. When she suddenly gets the chance to win back her future she knows she has to take it—whatever the cost.

She has no idea that shadows from a distant, haunted isle are watching her every move.

BOOK 2: TWO MOONS

Aboard the *Star of Deltora* with her three rivals for the Trader Rosalyn Apprenticeship, Britta knows that she has to keep her wits about her. She desperately wants to win the contest, but of course Jewel, Sky and Vashti feel the same, and one of them, she knows, is a ruthless enemy who will stop at nothing to succeed.

Britta is ready for trouble, but as the voyage fails to go as planned, and rumors of evil magic sweep her beloved ship, she starts to wonder if she has more to fear than simple human wickedness.

And nothing can prepare her for the terror that awaits her in the perilous, forbidden swamplands of Two Moons.